WHATSOEVER IS JUST

Whatsoever is Just

Published by The Conrad Press in the United Kingdom 2020

Tel: +44(0)1227 472 874
www.theconradpress.com
info@theconradpress.com

ISBN 978-1-913567-00-2

Typesetting and Cover Design by: Charlotte Mouncey, www.bookstyle.co.uk

The Conrad Press logo was designed by Maria Priestley.

Printed and bound in Great Britain by Clays Ltd, Elcograf S.p.A.

WHATSOEVER IS JUST

STUART HUTCHINSON

To Dorothy

1

'Turn the showers off,' chief inspector David Warne ordered, knowing it would be the fresh-faced PC who would have to step over the body into the powerful jets of water to reach the back wall of the wet-room.

They'd already photographed everything: Mark Farmwell-Pembury's naked body lying face down, water spraying the lower half of his legs, blood spiralling from his heart.

'Looks like a single stab wound,' Sarah Barnes, the pathologist, said, when she and her assistant had carefully turned the body over. 'Blade like a stiletto; he'd be dying as soon as it pierced his heart. Judging from the wound, the blade's been pulled out at an angle towards his right-hand side and the killer's left. The killer pulled the blade out and got out of the way as the body fell forward. All the bruising on the face is from when it hit the tiles. Six to seven hours ago, I'd guess. I'll be certain, when he's in the lab.'

Looking at any dead body, Warne still saw his wife, Clarice, lying in Sarah's lab ten months ago, following the hit and run ordained by Maurice Sewell from a cell in Belmarsh prison. Life changed forever, he saw himself standing over her in his red motor-bike leathers, after they'd cut the cleaner leathers, and all her clothes, off her, and covered her with a sheet.

'Killed this morning,' he said to Sarah, determinedly focussing on Mark Farmwell-Pembury. 'Call came in from his cleaner at ten past nine, just over an hour ago.'

'Special this,' he said to himself, as soon as the message reached his desk in Canterbury. Everybody knew the Farmwell-Temburys were one of the county's most prominent families. Instantly, he phoned the chief constable's office in Maidstone and put a team together. Siren blaring, blue-light flashing in the Monday morning February gloom, DS Liz Ezeoke-Bruce, now in the lounge with the cleaner, cut through the city's crawling traffic like a *Grand Prix* driver starting from the back of the grid. She hurtled the two of them to picture-postcard Chilham, the village seven miles from Canterbury, where Mark Farmwell-Pembury, an heir with his younger sister, Gillian, to the family's farming and brewing fortune in Kent, and land and industrial wealth in Lancashire, lived alone in a luxurious dwelling trans-formed from two late nineteenth-century semi-detached villas.

'We need to find Mark's car,' Liz said, as Warne returned to the designer-furnished lounge, still strewn with the debris of Mark's fiftieth birthday party on Saturday night.

'Aston Martin DB7?'

'That's it. The cleaner brought me a photo from Mark's desk, him and the car, a framed present from the dealer; personal plate, MRK 1. She says the car always stands at the side of the house on the paved area under the pergola. The killer probably took off in it.'

'He's ours, if he's still in it. No hiding in a car like that. Phone the station. Get them to organise a search. God knows how we're going to find evidence here, sifting through all this rubbish from Saturday night's party.'

'The cleaner only does light work; did some Sunday after-noon. She came in this morning to let in a professional firm with all their gear; steam-cleaners and chemicals. I've just cancelled that.'

'Great.'

'There's more.'

'Yeah?'

'No sign of a break-in, the cleaner says. The door was just closed on its latch. Security lock wasn't engaged. Alarm system was off.'

'So the killer was let in, or brought in, by Mark. Could be one of his pick-ups.'

'Dover patrol, a man off the ferry?'

'Could be. Or it's somebody Mark knows, somebody who has a key to the house and knows the code for the alarm. We need to find out who has keys.'

'I've already asked the cleaner. She only knows of one other person as well as herself who might have a key. It's a Vincent Clements, who was Mark's lover for about fifteen years. And you know what? The cleaner tells me there's a paper-knife missing from Mark's desk; thin blade, about ten inches long, with an ornamental handle, all metal; a present, specially made in Marrakech, from the same Vincent Clements.'

'Clements' Antiques, Sandwich, Tunbridge Wells, Tenterden. Best antique shops in Kent. When you've lived here longer, you'll buy something from them. Phone Sandwich straight-away. That's where Clements lives. Find out where he was last night.'

Leaving Liz to make her calls, he contacted Maidstone again to keep the bosses up to speed. He was put through to assistant chief constable Cunningham, appointed at the time of Clarice's murder. Three years Warne's junior, minor public school, married with three kids, father a knighted civil servant,

Warne saw immediately he was on heat to score big.

'Why you getting nowhere with the killing of DCI Warne's wife?' he demanded on his first visit to Canterbury nick last May. 'Maurice Sewell should be nailed for it, no question, even though he's inside. You haven't even found the car. Crime against one of our own; you're making us look like losers!'

'We're checking every car-breaker's yard in Kent, Sussex, and into London and Essex,' Warne countered, 'every likely garage that might have fixed a Mondeo with a damaged wing.'

'We need some luck,' a DC muttered, as Cunningham was on his way out.

'Get some,' Cunningham barked, turning round to face them all again.

Now, on the phone, he challenged, 'Be sure you get this right, Warne.'

'We're on it. I'm on my way to Mark's parents, Sir Christopher and Lady Farmwell-Pembury. I'll call at Mark's sister, Gillian Edmondson. She lives here in Chilham, about twenty minutes walk from Mark's house. I'm expecting she'll come with me to her parents' place, Nystole, four miles away.'

Local knowledge Cunningham might not have.

He brought everybody together in the lounge.

'The Farmwell-Pemburys don't know about Mark's death yet. I'm just on my way to tell them. So everybody schtum, until the body's been formally identified, and there's a formal announcement. Anybody leaks anything, they'll answer to me, personally.'

He let that sink in, before gesturing towards Liz. 'More people are coming. When they're here, DS Ezeoke-Bruce will organise a finger-tip search of this house and the immediate surrounding area, and there'll be some door to door. There'll be massive publicity about this case, locally and nationally. We all need to be at the top of our game.'

To Liz he said, 'I'll come back here when I've finished with the Farmwell-Pemburys. I'll drive there with a WPC.'

'Clements Antiques,' she replied. 'I've been in touch. Vincent Clements has been in Marrakech since November.'

'I bet he didn't take his key with him. Do we know where it is? Are we really sure nobody else has one?'

Could be a gay-basher, he said to himself, as he slid into the passenger seat of one of the cars parked alongside the wall of Chilham's Jacobean castle. Then he recollected the public disagreement (row on Mark's part) between Mark and his sister Gillian over the sale of a nineteenth century brewery building belonging to the family, near the West Railway Station in Canterbury. Mark, he recalled, had wanted the building more or less preserved as a themed restaurant, but Gillian, a chartered accountant, and the brains behind Farmwell-Pembury in Kent for well over a decade, though always withdrawn, had seen the building's immense potential for fundamental re-development as luxury apartments, and she'd won. All Mark had as consolation prize was the London builders he and his father, unusually allied, insisted on for the conversion, rather than the local Kent builders favoured by Gillian.

Nothing there for Gillian to have a murderous grudge about, Warne thought, even though the London builders were labelled 'cowboys' by the Kent firm.

Since Clarice's death, he'd considered quitting his large four-bedroom family house in Canterbury and moving into one of the Maltings apartments himself. Liz already lived there, alone, in one of the more affordable, one-bedroomed apartments with windows looking onto the railway lines. She was the only non-white person in the entire complex.

Life changed forever.

For what?

Two days ago he'd been in London on the demo against the invasion of Iraq.

Saturday, 15th February, 2003, the largest political demonstration London had ever seen.

Millions across the world also protesting against the invasion.

Pissing in the wind.

Blair wouldn't bat an eyelid.

In too deep with Bush.

2

From behind the half-opened front door, Gillian Edmondson's pale, strained face peered at them.

'Good morning, Mrs Edmondson,' Warne responded, hesitantly. 'I'm Chief Inspector David Warne, Canterbury CID, and this is WPC Emily Graham. May we come in? I'm afraid we have some very bad news. Perhaps we could all meet inside with you and your husband.'

'My husband's away, visiting his old college in Cambridge,' she said immediately, the door still half opened. Then, as if her statements would resolve any possible issue, she added, 'We are shortly to leave for New Zealand to visit his family. His father is very ill.'

'Please let us come inside,' Warne insisted. 'It's terrible news about your brother Mark, and we need to tell your parents.'

'Oh, Mark!'

She opened the door wide, showing them into the large oak-panelled hall of the detached house, which stood amid landscaped gardens. Modern, Warne said to himself, when they parked alongside a dirty, white Ford Focus with a dent in the offside wing; made to look older, like some of the houses in the village square.

He came straight to the point.

'Mrs Edmondson, Mark's dead, I'm afraid; killed by someone. His cleaner found his body this morning and phoned us immediately. We need to tell your parents.'

'Mark! No! No! No!'

She sat down on a settle, covering her face with her hands and bowing her head, her slight body tensely curved. Warne had expected to find her at home, because it was well known she'd become reclusive and semi-retired over the last few years. He knew too she was in her late forties, two or three years older than himself. Looking down on her now from his own sturdy six feet, however, he sensed he was seeing a woman under-nourished in every part of her being, a woman energised mainly by her own intensity. He saw again her brother's body lying in the wet-room; how sleek it had appeared, and on its way to plumpness, full of easy living. Gillian, in her brown top and brown trousers, her short black hair pierced with grey, her finger-nails bitten to the quick, seemed as ascetic as a saint. However many millions she had secured for her family, she apparently derived little pleasure from them, though people in Kent knew her marriage to Ralph Edmondson, who brought his family's New Zealand winery into the alliance, had substantially augmented the family fortune.

'Mrs Edmondson,' Warne asked after a minute or two. 'Is there anyone in the house to get you something? Can we get you something?'

'No, you're right,' she responded, looking up at him, her face suddenly decisive and emptied of emotion, though there had been no tears. 'We must tell my parents immediately. I'll get ready.'

She disappeared into a room behind the hall staircase.

'I'll drive myself,' she announced, when she re-appeared, shapelessly concealed in a long, grey overcoat and a head-scarf. 'You can follow me.'

'I've often walked past Nystole,' Warne assured her, as they followed her to the Focus. 'I know where it is.'

Which was as well, since she lost them, as soon as she turned out of her drive.

'She's driving like a mad woman,' WPC Graham said from behind the wheel. 'Single-track lane, blind corners, she's touched sixty. She could have a head-on. Crazy!'

Warne didn't bother to respond. Wiping the passenger window, he looked out at the bare apple and pear orchards, and the hop fields. Since moving to Canterbury, Clarice and he had regularly walked in this area, usually in late springtime, when the season's arousal was well underway, and there was blossom everywhere. The last time was with a group of friends. Passing Nystole, they'd climbed the Downs, stopping half way to gaze back at the great house, which was originally sixteen century, though much extended since.

'There you are,' he said to Clarice, gesturing towards the house and smiling at her, loving the pink colour the climb brought to her face, '*The past is never dead. It's not even past.*'

'What are you talking about?' one of their friends asked.

'Oh, it's David's English degree,' Clarice replied, slightly mocking, as she sipped water from a plastic bottle. 'He's never got over it. He's quoting William Faulkner. You know, the American novelist, from the American South, Mississippi. David wrote a long essay on Faulkner in his final year, but Faulkner was never my Oxford cup of tea.'

Now, typically, she'd turned the mockery on herself. She'd done English at Oxford, while he was at Leeds. As they surveyed Nystole from the Downs, however, he knew she was aware it wasn't Faulkner he was actually thinking about. It was the fact that the owner of Nystole, Christopher Farmwell-Pembury, before being knighted by Mrs Thatcher for services to the Conservative cause, originated from his and Clarice's own past. He came from Atherstone in Lancashire, the town ten miles north-west of Manchester, where they were both born, and where for two hundred years or more the Farmwell-Pembury money was made from coal, nails, nuts and bolts, and, finally from their cotton-mill, with its name, 'PROSPERO'S', vainly lettered in white capitals on its chimney; members of both their families having been Farmwell-Pembury employees.

'The bits of the past Thatcher wants to chuck away will take with them the bits she wants to keep,' he remembered saying to Clarice in the early years of their marriage, as they looked at photographs of their grandparents, who had gone to the same schools in Atherstone. It was when he was in the Met in London, and Mrs Thatcher, the prime-minister, was their MP in Finchley, and they clustered forlornly at Labour Party meetings, because, unless you were a Farmwell-Pembury, or "a boss's man," or someone wanting to set yourself apart, like his mother and her sister, aunty Lucy, how could you not vote Labour if you came from Atherstone? Then Warne got a transfer to the CID in Kent, and, awaiting them, was Christopher Farmwell-Pembury himself. He'd moved to the county at the end of the 1940s, when he married Penelope Fincham, an heiress to the Fincham farming, brewery, and pub fortune.

No letting the past die now, Warne was thinking, as WPC Graham turned into Nystole's drive. It's all I have of Clarice.

They parked alongside the Focus on a large expanse of gravel to the front and sides of the house, the gravel itself embraced by large areas of lawn which eventually became pasture supporting great oaks and beeches. Surveying these grounds, Warne thought some more of the past. He wondered how true the rumours were that, nearly fifty years ago, in the sixties, cars filled with senior military figures and senior Conservative politicians, active and retired, had arrived during darkness at Nystole to plan a possible coup against Harold Wilson's Labour government. He knew Sir Christopher had powerfully championed Mrs Thatcher during the Falklands campaign and the '84 miners' strike, and two weeks ago, after a period of absence from the programme, had suddenly re-appeared on the BBC's *Question Time* to deliver unqualified support for 'Great Britain's participation, alongside our ally the United States of America,' in the looming war against Saddam Hussein's Iraq. Every time another panellist said 'the UK,' Sir Christopher had countered with an emphatic 'Great Britain,' and when it was implied he was a mere armchair general with nothing personal at stake, he had proudly announced that his granddaughter's fiancé, a captain in the army, was ready 'to do his duty and serve in Iraq, whenever his country called on him.'

Crusaders like Sir Christopher are swinging it for Blair and Iraq, Warne thought, getting out of the car; especially when they were Thatcherites. Blair's a crusader himself.

Gillian, whose daughter Caroline was the granddaughter Sir Christopher referred to, was waiting for them at Nystole's Gothic entrance porch. She led them into a spacious hall with a grand central staircase half way down its length. Opening the first door on the left to reveal a library-cum-office, she said, 'You can wait in here. Nowadays my father's secretary only comes on Tuesdays and Thursdays. I'll bring my parents.'

The library was furnished with chairs and sofas in warm,

wine-coloured leather. A light blinked from IT equipment on one of the oak tables.

Warne and WPC Graham went to look out of one of the tall windows giving on to the gravel, lawn, and pasture-land, the last reaching to the edge of the Downs. They turned, when Gillian eventually entered the room with her parents.

'My daughter has already told us the dreadful news, chief inspector,' Sir Christopher began immediately, not bothering with introductions, and gesturing everyone to take a seat. 'I assume,' he continued grimly, 'there's not much more you can tell us at this stage.'

Traces of the North in his voice were sometimes thought to give him an edge over 'Southerners,' but Warne knew they could hold no advantage over his own accent, as he replied, 'No, sir; I'm afraid there is no more I can tell you at this stage.'

He was aware Lady Penelope's eyes were full of tears, so he didn't immediately continue; but then, feeling he had to convey a sense of purpose, he said, 'We're searching for your son's car, and for the weapon that killed him.'

'Oh no,' Lady Penelope gasped, one hand covering her eyes with a handkerchief, as her daughter moved to sit on the arm of her chair and hold her other hand.

'Perhaps you should leave me to deal with this, my dear,' her husband said protectively.

From Atherstone stories Warne knew Christopher Farmwell-Pembury had returned to the town in 1946 as a much decorated war hero, following battles in the deserts of North Africa, Sicily, and the whole length of Italy. Now, nearly sixty years later, and in his eighties, he still looked unflinching, as he must have looked when commanding men to initiate, or repel, any attack.

His full head of blond hair, passed on to Mark, turning silvery grey, he was dressed impressively in a navy blue double-breasted blazer, pale-blue shirt, yellow patterned tie with matching handkerchief hanging loosely from his breast pocket, light grey trousers, and brown leather brogues. Powerful in various companies and the Bank of England, as well as Farmwell-Pembury enterprises, he'd governed people's life chances for over half a century, and even now, in his eighties, betrayed little sign that mortality might be governing him.

'I must stay to hear everything,' Lady Penelope said, dabbing her eyes.

Warne didn't expect her to remember him, but he'd once managed to sit next to her during a Canterbury University town-gown PR dinner a dozen or so years ago, when he'd represented the police, and Clarice local school teachers. Talking to her on that occasion, he'd been charmed by her delight that he'd not only heard of Atherstone, where her husband's family was from, but had actually been born there. He'd seen her husband's male friends attending on her and diverting her, as if they were knights at the round table. Slight as her daughter, she exuded none of Gillian's intense self-repression. On what would have been a routine Monday morning she too, like her husband, was dressed with care, and even for performance, in a grey wool skirt, a lavender cashmere cardigan and sweater, and matching pearl necklace and earrings. Expensively cut and dyed, her hair curled up just above her shoulders, like a young girl's.

'I expect one of us needs formally to identify the body,' Sir Christopher said.

'Yes,' Warne replied, sensing the pressure Sir Christopher habitually applied to people, but aware too of Lady Penelope's silent weeping.

'When would you want me to do that,' Sir Christopher continued.

'I think as soon as possible will be best. We may well be ready this afternoon, or perhaps this evening. We can only formally announce the death after the identification. I'm sure your family will want to establish some control over publicity. For our part we'll protect your family as much as we can by keeping a tight hold on everything.'

'I'll inform our solicitors and our publicity people immediately,' Sir Christopher said. 'One of them will accompany me, and we will come to see my son's body as soon as you contact us.'

'Meanwhile, I have to ask you to think of any enemies your son might have had.'

'Enemies of my son! What could we possibly know about matters such as that, chief inspector?'

Back in the car WPC Graham accelerated powerfully away from Nystole, causing the gravel to rattle the car's underside. '

As far as Sir Christopher's concerned,' she said, 'us women might as well not exist.'

'Hmm,' Warne grunted. He knew Sir Christopher had always been a womaniser, who despised Mark's homosexuality.

3

In Chilham, he went straight to the fourteenth century pub for a cheese and chutney sandwich and a pint of Fincham's best bitter.

'Lovely pint,' he said to the publican, while he waited for his sandwich.

'You in charge of what's happening,' the publican protested, 'whole village taped shut. I'm losing custom.'

He moved with his pint and sandwich to a small isolated table and a high-backed seat by the fire.

'Farmwell-Pembury: F-P, Fuck-n-Pee,' he muttered to himself, biting into his sandwich, and remembering men grabbing their dicks, women their crotches, jerking their hips backwards and forwards; a rebellious Atherstone chant in the mines, the nut and bolt works, and in Prospero's, the cotton-mill; the chant dying-out now, but still filtering into school playgrounds when he was a child, though some people always bowed and scraped to the Farmwell-Pemburys, as if they were royalty; cleaned and served for them; his job now after this killing.

'They wouldn't give me mi money!'

His dad's bitter complaint, lasting from the forties, when he'd laid paving slabs in the entrance courtyard to Prospero's.

His mother's instant response, 'I've told you. I don't want that family's name mentioned in this house.'

Her near panic taking her immediately upstairs to her

bedroom, its door closing firmly.

Resentfully, his dad, 'Flagger Bill,' persisting with his griev-
ance. 'Just after t`war, I was tryin` to get mi business back on
its feet, nursin` mi first wife. They made me wait over three
months. We were skint.'

Labour-voting class antagonism.

Something else (what?) from his mother, who'd had a
breakdown at nineteen, when she worked as an office girl at
Prospero's. Like aunty Lucy, her protective older sister, she
refused to vote for anybody, though his dad said they were,
'Born Tories, both of `em.'

Where did class struggles get you?

Nowhere, according to Blair.

The F-Ps hadn't killed Clarice.

That was down to Maurice Sewell, criminal class, if any class;
brought up in violent destitution in Ramsgate, till he was big
enough to break the jaw of his wife-beating father and throw
him out of what passed for a house.

Sewell haunting him all through his police career; Chief
Superintendent Joe Pawsey in the Met insisting he and three
other detectives dance to Sewell's tune.

'Clarice, I'm done. I don't know where to turn.'

'Leave. Be a good copper somewhere else. I'll teach somewhere else.'

Good copper in Canterbury, he put Sewell away for drugs-
and gun-running, money-laundering, prostitution.

Then he kills the love of your life.

'He strikes back.'

Clarice's own words, five years ago, reading a story in *The
Observer* allegedly connecting Sewell to a spate of murderous

violence, following the suicide of his son, Paul, under a train at Waterloo International.

Plenty of striking back and killing in Iraq soon, he thought, swallowing the last of his sandwich and drinking deeply into his pint; revenge for 9/11, Bush satisfying basic instinct. Where's my basic instinct? Do I have any? Compassionate leave after Clarice is murdered, and I'm back on the job, back to normal, because I'm always fucking normal. I'm expected to be normal.

Abruptly he stood up, downing the rest of his beer. He met Liz as soon as he was back at the crime scene.

'We've found the car and somebody in it,' she announced.

'Great, and?'

'It's a student, a Danny Barratt, asleep in the car in a super-market car park in Reading, his home town.'

'You're going to tell me he spent the night with Mark.'

Liz paused, as if he was spoiling her story, so he nodded for her to carry on.

'We'll get Danny's formal statement as soon as we have him in Canterbury,' she said, 'but he's already told a Thames Valley unit that Mark picked him up around ten on Sunday night in Dover, where he'd just got off the ferry from Calais. They drove to the house in Chilham, had sex, all of it consensual. Then he falls asleep in Mark's bed, wakes up for a pee in the *en-suite*, wanders downstairs and finds Mark in the wet-room as we found him. He takes off in the car, because he's scared to death.'

'When will he be back in Canterbury?'

'Him and his dad, and the car should arrive around seven. Thames Valley's already had him thoroughly examined, and all his clothes bagged up.'

'Right. We'll have him examined again and get a statement as soon as he arrives.'

'Thames Valley says it's already been terrible for his family. The dad, a prominent local headmaster, had to be hauled out of his school. Mother's also a teacher, and there's a sister, sixteen. They'd no idea the lad was gay.'

'It could get a whole lot worse for them.'

'And for the Farmwell-Pemburys; how did you get on with them?'

Pausing for a moment, Warne then said, 'You don't get on with Sir Christopher, unless you inhabit his world, or pretend to. I just gave information and received information. Sir Christopher will identify the body as soon as we're ready. As far as he's concerned, we're put on this earth to do what he thinks has to be done.'

'Hello! Am I hearing some politics again?'

'I'm sure you'll always keep me in check, Liz.'

'We'll see. Anyway the body's already left for the mortuary. It could be identified later today.'

'I'll let Sir Christopher know. He'll want to keep a lid on things, so let's try to be tight ourselves. If we screw up, Sir Christopher will crucify us. He always loathed Mark's gayness.'

'Tight's going to be difficult in a place like this. I've already had villagers in my ear. Some of them team-up with the cleaner for routine cleaning sessions at the house. They've worked out something terrible has happened to Mark. They all know he cruises the docks at Dover, picking up young men for a night, then driving them away early in the morning to catch a train from Ashford International.'

'I was expecting that to come out. So what do you think? If

the paper-knife was the weapon, has this Danny Barratt shoved it into Mark because of hatred, or self-hatred, fear of ever facing his headmaster father?'

'Whoa! The lad's not said anything against Mark; not that we know of at least.'

'Not yet.'

'Perhaps the lad will tell us why Mark used the wet-room and not the *en-suite*.'

'Consideration for the lad; didn't want to wake him up; likes to use the wet-room?'

'Could be.'

He could see Liz had everything under control in Chilham. In what remained of daylight coppers were crawling over the cottage and the immediate surroundings. Door to door had started, not revealing what had happened, but asking if neighbours had been aware of anything unusual during the night. There was nothing more for him to do at the crime scene, so he decided to take one of the unmarked cars and drive back to Canterbury and prepare for the arrival of Danny Barratt. He knew Liz would welcome being left in charge, and he had complete confidence in her. He'd worked with her for just over a year and had already told her she would have his full support in her bid for further promotion to detective inspector.

4

L iz likes digging at what she sees as my politics, he thought in the car. She knew that two days ago, on Saturday, he'd been in London on the big demo against the invasion of Iraq. Some said two million protesters; a mass of people diverging from one another in all sorts of ways, like soldiers in any army, members of any political party.

'You lost, 2 nil.'

A boy, about ten, him and his dad, wearing Arsenal scarves and hats, joining the demo at nearly half-past three, fresh from watching the lunchtime cup game (United v Arsenal) on TV; recognising his Manchester United hat, pulled low over his forehead and ears against the cold, and the many police cameras.

'Thanks,' he responded. 'I'm videoing the game for later. I didn't want to know the result.'

'Sorry,' the dad said. 'Giggsy missed a sitter. But we played you off the park. I hear Blair's turning to Fergie for advice on leadership. He should give Arsène Wenger a bell instead.'

He let that go. With Clarice he voted enthusiastically for Blair in 1997 and again in 2001, two years ago. But now, like an evangelist, Blair was supporting Bush's ignoramus war plans against Saddam Hussein. Declaring their party membership, they'd sent him a joint letter urging restraint. Always he'd see Clarice posting the letter, as they left on the motorbike for what became the fatal week-end to Ypres and Lille, last April. Blair had just returned from meeting Bush in Texas.

'Cry God for Tony, England, and St George,' she exclaimed bleakly, as she dropped the letter into the post-box and returned to sit behind him on the bike. 'Is that how Blair's appealing to us? Kosovo's gone to his head.'

'We did think it was a triumph when Blair got Clinton involved in Kosovo,' he said over his shoulder to her.

'I know. But once a saviour's not always a saviour. Anyway, what are we saving in Iraq?'

Father Nigerian, mother English, Liz, in her late twenties, kept him mindful of other areas of the world where Britain had fucked up, and where there were violent power struggles, whether any ex-colonial power still fucked up or not. He could see she found an identity in her police career, even as he also sensed her resistance to a white world only relating to her in this allowed role. Recalling triumphant *Match of the Day* images of Nigerian football stars Jay-Jay Ochocha and Nwanko Kanu, he wondered if they also experienced this conflict.

'Racism comes off some British white people like an energy,' Liz had said to him. They were taking a coffee back to their car, and Stephen Lawrence, murdered by white youths ten years ago only because he was black, was again on the front pages. Clicking open the central locking, she added, 'but not off you.'

'Thank Christ for that,' he retorted, wondering again, as Liz started the car, if he should have been more outspoken about racism, when he was in the Met. At university he'd written a ten thousand word essay on 'Faulkner's Southern Heritage of Slavery', becoming more aware, as he did so, of the entire US being blighted by racism, and of British fortunes, British cities (Bristol, Liverpool, Glasgow) founded on the slave trade. He knew he hadn't contributed explicitly to the Met's being 'institutionally racist,' the judgement delivered over its bungled handling of the Stephen Lawrence case, but he had kept his head down. I was in my twenties, he told himself, first job. I had Joe Pawsey all over me; wanting me in on dirty deals with Maurice Sewell.

A week after the exchange over the coffee, Liz told him some of her family history. Glancing at *The Guardian* on his desk, with its headlines about Bush and Blair and Iraq, she asked, 'Suppose it all goes wrong?'

When he didn't answer, she began to tell him how her Nigerian grandfather returned to Nigeria in the fifties, all fired-up by the civil rights movement during his university education in the States. 'He flung himself into Nigerian nationalism and the struggle for independence from Britain,' she said, 'but then lost two of his sons in civil wars killing millions. In the end, because he had become a successful general, he made his fortune from protecting western oil interests during the military juntas.'

'Complicated,' he remembered replying, feebly.

'My father,' Liz went on, was the third son. He came to Manchester University in England as a postgraduate student, had a relationship with my mother, a librarian, and here I am. All through school, till I was about twelve, I was asked, "Why are you not white like your mummy?".'

'Parents still together?'

Liz smiled. 'No chance. He'd had his white woman, revenge perhaps; she her black man, just for the experience, I think. She'd become a mother, and the only other thing she wanted was to become a head librarian. While she was bringing me up, I saw she only had relationships with men, when she needed them.'

'Your father?'

'Had a Nigerian wife and three children. Then, when Babangida's coup came along, he resisted it and was killed by a mail bomb.'

'Bloody hell!'

Human beings expendable, war or no war, he thought, as he now sat in a traffic jam around Canterbury's Roman city wall; how Maurice Sewell saw Clarice, and maybe how Mark Farmwell-Pembury's killer saw him. He glanced at the tips of hundreds of daffodils beginning their annual emergence in the wide grass verge; nature's indifferent recurrence.

Inching forward, he moved into the outside lane to prepare for his right turn at the Riding Gate Roundabout. A driver in a Nissan, in the slower left hand lane, both hands clenched and pulling on his steering wheel, was moving manically up and down in his seat, as if to lift his car up and above the cars in front of him. Looking fixedly ahead, he raised the middle finger of his right hand at Warne.

'You'll get yours.'

Maurice Sewell's threat, as he stood in the dock three years ago. In his sixties and pared down to the bone, a large silver cross hanging on his breast, he was wearing his now habitual black track-suit. As if along the barrel of a loaded gun, he sighted along his pointing finger at Warne.

His trial finished, Warne knew he was indicating that he, Maurice Sewell, remained as much in control as ever. Already, since the death of his son five years ago, he'd adopted his mother's Roman Catholicism and begun living like a monk. His cell inside would only be an exchange for his cells outside, in any one of his properties. There, he would continue withdrawing into essentials and final, God-like, avenging judgements, knowing he would always have the money, and therefore the power, for whatever the judgements took.

'Anybody in a uniform can be bought, your honour,' he insinuatingly assured the judge, speaking man to man, as his left hand fingered the silver cross. It was as if 'being bought' was something the judge, in his own uniform and line of work, must be all too familiar with.

'He'll consider it an apostasy you've arrested him,' Clarice said.

For over a decade a dedicated Kent CID team had been on Sewell's case, raiding his millionaire's converted oast house near Sissinghurst, and jetting off to stake out his housing compound on the *Costa del Sol.* Always, the team found nothing. Only when Warne was asked by the chief constable's office to review the case was Sewell reeled in.

Knowing he was a Kent lad who'd used Ramsgate's marina for his yacht, Warne instigated a search of Sewell's ex-second wife's house in the town. There, in various cellar-rooms, he found consignments of guns, drugs, and money, together with papers recording payment for dozens of Eastern European and African girls. On this evidence, he arrested Sewell when, offering his austere look to the world, he next arrived in Britain, stepping down at Ramsgate's Manston airport, from a cheap, crowded holiday flight from Spain, as if he couldn't care less whether or not the law decided even to notice him.

'Be fucking careful, Davy boy. That's all I'm saying. Maurice never forgets.'

Ominous, almost touching, words from Joe Pawsey, now retired, phoning from his house in Chalfont St Giles, Buckinghamshire, when Sewell's arrest was all over the media.

'You're the son Pawsey never had,' Clarice used to joke.

Be 'Davy boy' on Pawsey's bent team, she'd still be alive.

Someday he'd drag Pawsey by his balls from Chalfont St Giles.

He was sure it was a Mondeo that hit Clarice. He'd seen it in the bike's mirrors, immediately behind them, after they came off the motorway in Wincheap, returning towards midnight from their trip to Ypres and Lille. The Mondeo had followed them to the Wincheap Roundabout, overlooked by the city's ruin of a Norman castle, and turned left behind them, as they moved onto the ring road. At St Peter's Roundabout, it had again tailed them onto a deserted Rheims Way. There, in the forty mile limit, he remembered holding the bike at thirty to encourage the Mondeo to pass, but it closed in behind, until he signalled for the right turn at the next roundabout. Then, flooring the accelerator, the driver aimed the Mondeo straight into the bike, smashing it over before hurtling on towards London and oblivion.

He'd hit Clarice full on, violently pitching the bike onto the wide verge at the left-hand side of the road.

'Me! It should have been me! Another six inches you'd have got me,' Warne wailed into the empty night, scrambling on his knees, frantically unzipping Clarice's leathers to feel for her heart, already knowing it would never beat again.

Only in the mortuary, deranged by the sight of Clarice's fatally broken body, her right leg, under the sheet, half-severed from it, did he understand she was always Sewell's intended target.

'You'll get yours.'

Sewell sentencing him forever to a life without her.

Endless guilt.
Endless grief.

5

'I'm not a student,' Danny Barratt insisted, sitting in the interview room. 'I graduated two years ago with a first in French. 'I'm working in a gay bar in Paris. I was on my way home for a few days. I was going to come out to my parents. But now,' he added, 'that's been done for me.'

Unlikely gay-basher, if true, Warne thought, before asking reflexively, 'What's this bar called?'

'*L'Arbre de Connaissance*, Tree of Knowledge. It's in *Place Pigalle*. Its sign is a big bright tree, made out in lights, loaded with luscious fruits. They'll vouch for me. I've been there since November.'

His father had come with him from Reading, but, after his medical examination, he'd insisted on being interviewed alone, even declining a lawyer.

'Nothing to hide,' he declared to Warne and Liz on their way to the interview room, and wearing the baggy, grey track-suit Thames Valley had provided him with.

Confident sod, even though he's shorter than Liz, Warne said to himself, noting again the designer stubble complementing the thick, black bushy hair.

'Only that keeps this down, twice a day sometimes,' Danny remarked, caressing the stubble, when a cut throat razor was taken from his expensive leather toilet bag.

The examinations had revealed plenty of evidence on him of sex with Mark Farmwell-Pembury, and Warne and Liz had already seen footage from Dover ferry terminal showing the young man sliding into Mark's Aston Martin.

'Why did Mark shower in the wet room, when there was a shower in the luxury *en-suite* a few yards from his bed? Did you two have a row?'

Asking these questions, Warne knew there was no evidence on either body of a struggle. In any case, it would have been unequal. Mark would have overpowered Danny with one arm tied behind his back.

'I don't know why he went to the wet room, except it's more spacious, and you always get a better kind of shower in wet rooms. And there was no row, just great sex. I slept like a baby, till I had to have a pee.'

'Why was the house door only on the latch? Mark had an elaborate security lock and an alarm?'

'I don't know.'

'Tells us what happened, when you arrived at the house,' Liz said.

The young man paused, as if creating a picture for himself.

'Mark reversed the car onto the parking area at the side of the house. By the time I was at the front door, he was already opening it.'

'It just opened like a simple front door?' Liz interrupted. 'He didn't punch any buttons on the alarm system in the hall?'

'Not that I noticed.'

'Then what?' Warne demanded.

'Well, chief inspector, we both knew what we were there for. It wasn't the first time for either of us. Mark gestured at all the mess from his birthday party and asked if I wanted a drink, or anything. I said I was OK, so he told me how to get to the bedroom. He came up about fifteen minutes later. He went into the *en- suite* for another five minutes or so, and then, when I was dying for it, he came to me. And, let me tell you, chief inspector, there was nothing he didn't know.'

Silence, till Liz said, 'And you woke up to find him dead?'

'You want us to believe you didn't hear anything!' Warne challenged; 'somebody else coming into the house and killing him!'

'It's a big house. The wet room's at the back end, under the stairs.'

'You found the body and took off?' Liz said.

'I was scared out of my mind; seeing someone dead I'd just been in bed with. I'd never even seen a dead body before. But believe me or not, when the police found me in Reading, I was on the point of turning myself in. I'm intelligent enough to know I had to do that.'

'How do we know you didn't come across the killer?' Warne said. 'How do we know the killer hasn't threatened you to keep silent?'

'Look. I'm here to help. But I do want a lawyer, if we're going in that direction.'

'Forensics supports his story,' Liz said, when they were back in Warne's office.

'So far, but it's either him, or somebody else with a key; and maybe he did disturb the killer. I don't like that cut-throat, even though it's not the murder weapon. And his story's too straightforward.'

'Do you think he's involved in some sort of plot to kill Mark?'

'Good question. He's there in Dover to pick Mark up, rather than Mark picking him up. At the house he lets the killer in;

elaborate, but worth considering.'

'If the alarm was set, he'd have to know the combination to shut it off.'

'I don't entirely trust our Danny. He's hinting one night stands, out of nowhere, are a regular habit. But he's not stupid. He'll be aware of the risks he takes. He's bound to guard against them. That's what that cut-throat's all about. Self-protection, I'm sure.' Then he said, 'Somebody better phone that bar in Paris, check he works there.'

'I'll do it.'

'You can do it French!'

'*Oui, c'est très simple.*'

Minutes later, having sorted out the number, she was through to the bar, asking what he hoped he would have been able to ask himself, '*Est-ce que vous connaissez Monsieur Danny Barratt? Est-ce qu'il travaille chez vous depuis novembre?*'

'It's "*Oui*" to both questions,' she said.

So, two days later, they had to release Danny Barratt on bail.

'We've nothing to hold him on,' Warne insisted on the phone to an angry assistant chief constable Cunningham. 'And we're still crawling all over Mark's house and pulling in all his known gay lovers.'

'Be sure you keep the Farmwell-Pemburys on side,' Cunningham almost threatened. 'Sir Christopher thinks you're making too much of all this queer stuff, dragging his family into all that shit. He can damage all our chances, if you screw up.'

You mean all your fucking chances, Warne thought, turning to all the new paperwork on his desk: a mixed race American student beaten up by some local white youths; lead stolen from the roofs of local churches; fifty or so kids' bikes in a barn on a farm at Pett Bottom, advertised for sale in the local Canterbury paper, but apparently stolen from around London.

Towards lunch Danny Barratt's father arrived to take his son home. Clean shaven, greying black, trimmed hair, an older version of his son, Warne had met him briefly, when Danny first arrived from Reading, but they'd hardly spoken.

'If you have children, Mr Warne,' he now said sorrowfully, 'I hope you're more successful with them than I seem to have been with Danny. I'm mortified he couldn't reveal to me he was gay. I thought I was different from some of the parents I deal with. At school we often know more about young people's sexual inclinations than their parents do.'

'Well, perhaps being like other parents is some consolation,' Warne replied. 'But no, I don't have children myself.'

Not even photos any more, he reflected, remembering the black sister and brother, eleven and nine, Clarice and he were about to adopt, after they'd finally given up on the miseries of IVF; remembering too the letters from black activists in various social services accusing them of 'kidnapping black children in order to obliterate their black identity.'

'All we need,' he said to Clarice.

The desk sergeant knocked on his door, as soon as the Barratts had left.

'Assault on the American student,' he said. 'He's in hospital, badly beaten up, but nothing life-threatening. His dad's on his way over from Boston.'

Warne unearthed the file.

'Give this to DS Ezeoke-Bruce,' he said.

6

February passed into March, and they were still nowhere in finding Mark's killer. Assuming a lover might have unexpectedly arrived at Mark's cottage, found Danny Barratt in Mark's bed, and then killed Mark in a fit of jealousy, they'd traced likely candidates in the area, but all were in the clear, and anyway how had they got into Mark's house? Warne had seen Vincent Clements' key in the shop safe in Sandwich, where, according to the manager, who ran the entire enterprise throughout Kent, it had rested unmoved, 'for sentimental reasons,' for over ten years.

Back early from Morocco, Vincent was coming to see Warne at the station to offer any help he could. This appointment had been made for a Tuesday afternoon. In the morning, a meeting had been arranged for Warne and Liz at Nystole. They had no new information, but Cunningham demanded the Farmwell-Pemburys be attended to.

'As if the F-Ps are running the bleeding case,' Warne protested to Liz.

Mark's funeral had happened a week ago. Referring to his responsibility for the family's Fincham pub chain throughout Kent and Sussex and into London, a Farmwell-Pembury spokesman proclaimed him a kindly and generous person, who would typically give a lift to anyone.

'I bet he'd have left Naomi Campbell standing in the wind and rain,' Liz commented to Warne, as they left the crematorium.

Two days after the funeral Gillian Edmondson and her husband flew to New Zealand.

Then the invasion of Iraq began, Warne and Liz listening to news reports on its development as they drove on the Tuesday morning to Nystole. It was the same road alongside the river Stour they'd taken to find Mark's body, and again the day was gloomy, as if the sun couldn't be bothered to make an effort.

Let's hope we can soon come up with some light, Warne thought, before saying to Liz, 'While we hunt for one killer, our government's more than ready to kill by the hundreds, if not thousands. We're still up to our necks in Afghanistan.'

Seeing 'Shock and Awe' on TV news, he wondered if Bush and Blair ever asked themselves what it would be like for their own loved ones to be on the receiving end of so murderous an onslaught. Had they accepted, at least implicitly, that Iraqi lives didn't count for much; that you could kill an Iraqi family, and it would be worth it? Decide someone's an 'enemy', you could do what you liked with them; kill them before they killed you, so the argument always went. Not entirely different from Maurice Sewell's belief in eliminating rivals and maintaining supremacy, though he was actually a kind of Saddam Hussein, a London strong man, violently protecting his interests and sometimes, so Joe Pawsey claimed, even aiding the law.

'Arabs, Islam,' Liz commented, as if reading Warne's mind. 'Do you think we'd have "Shock and Awe" against white Christians? What happened to, *As we forgive them that trespass against us*? We said it every morning at my Church of England Schools. And what happens in Iraq after Saddam? I've read Sunnis and Shias would be at each other's throats but for him.'

'I've heard Bush didn't even know there are Sunnis and Shias.'

From the passenger seat he gazed through the grey gloom towards the Stour's oblivious water meadows. Good copper? How good did events ever allow you to be? You were implicated in this war, simple as that; blood on your hands.

'You and me,' he said, 'try to make justice happen, supposedly so we don't become anything like an Iraq. But before the invasion began, I saw on TV people sitting at street cafés in Baghdad, like Canterbury in summer. Few women, but they all seemed happy enough. What right have we to destroy that?'

Liz not responding, he went on. 'Sometimes I think all that justifies one system over another is if fewer dead bodies are needed to maintain it. Forget so-called morality. Let's keep people alive. Let's ask ourselves how many people are worth killing to have system A instead of system B. Trouble is, you can never do the reckoning, especially in advance, and wars of invasion are as old as the hills.'

'For now,' Liz said, 'let's concentrate on the one dead body we can count.'

At Nystole they were again shown into the library-cum-office. Lady Penelope, in a pale grey trouser suit, greeted them from the table bearing the IT equipment. Removing her glasses, she came towards them to shake their hands, before saying, 'All the writing on that screen has suddenly gone very small. I can hardly read it.'

'Perhaps you need to go into "Tools" or something,' Liz volunteered.

'All Greek to me,' Lady Penelope replied.

Sir Christopher entered, acknowledging his visitors with a grunt. Wearing a light brown tweed jacket, again with matching tie and handkerchief, he went to gaze into the mist through one of the long windows.

A girl, about seventeen, came in bringing coffee and tea and biscuits. As soon as she said, 'Miwk,' Warne knew she was local.

Sir Christopher wanted neither coffee nor tea.

'Would you like me to help you with the computer,' Liz suggested to Lady Penelope.

'Well, if you think you can I would be very grateful. My husband's secretary won't be here till tomorrow.'

'Along with her degrees, DS Ezeoke-Bruce has a high level IT Diploma,' Warne offered, encouragingly.

'Ezeoke-Bruce!' Sir Christopher exclaimed from his position at the window. 'Why not Bruce-Ezeoke, or just Bruce?'

'Or just Ezeoke,' Liz challenged. 'But I wanted my Nigerian name and my English name.'

Ignoring the explanation, as Liz and Lady Penelope moved towards the table where the computer was, Sir Christopher turned towards Warne. He seemed glad to get the women out of the way.

Careful not to spill his coffee, Warne moved to join him at the window.

'I see, chief inspector, you have been pursuing your inquiries in homosexual circles,' Sir Christopher began.

'Yes, that was clearly a move we had to make. We've been in contact with all Mark's known acquaintances.'

'You've released the young man who supposedly spent a night with my son. Why shouldn't the murder inquiry now be pursued in other, more orthodox, directions?'

'We're looking in all directions, but the young man did sleep with Mark. He's made a statement to that effect. He drove off in Mark's car.'

His contempt at the ready, Sir Cristopher addressed the grey-ness through the window, 'Homosexuals are always unreliable. I'm sure we can agree on that.'

'You're saying your son was unreliable?'

'Mr Warne, I've long recognised that it has been my daughter, Gillian, who has held our family business together and been responsible for its commercial success, even though she retreats from all publicity.'

'I do have colleagues who are gay,' Warne insisted. 'They're as good as anyone else.'

'Gay!' Looking into the mist, as if its ambiguity signalled everything that was wrong with the modern world, Sir Christopher found more contempt. 'What about treachery, the Cambridge traitors, Burgess, Blunt? Nothing "gay" about treachery. And in the war we had to keep them down; men becoming women, useless in an army, when you have to know who you are; whom you're with.'

Jesus, am I really having this conversation, Warne asked himself. Your son's been murdered, for Christ's sake. Thousands are about to die in Iraq. Maybe your granddaughter's fiancé will die. Who cares if any one of them fancies a man or a woman? My God, only to have the person you love in your arms!

'Not all the Cambridge spies were homosexual,' he held his ground. 'And it's just the way some people live. I have to tell you the real danger in Mark's case was his promiscuity. He took enormous risks with his health and personal safety.'

'Hmm.'

The fucker's deciding I can't give him the game he wants, can't even knock the ball back Warne concluded. He sure as hell doesn't want to talk about promiscuity. I bet he'll bad-mouth me to Cunningham.

Happy noises came from the computer.

'I've fixed everything at pitch fourteen for you,' Warne heard Liz say. 'It's what I use. And here's my card, if you ever want to contact me directly.'

'The writing on the screen is so clear,' Lady Penelope exclaimed.

Sick of talking to Sir Christopher and sure there would be no profit in referring to Vincent Clements' impending visit, Warne turned towards the two women.

'Mr Warne,' Lady Penelope said, 'we are so grateful you have both come to see us, just to keep in contact with us. It's such a help, after Mark's terrible murder. And I do want to say I'm aware of your own sorrow over your wife's death in that appalling hit and run traffic accident.'

'Thank you,' Warne said.

'I remember too that we have met before, at that university dinner. What was it, ten or fifteen years ago?'

'Nearer fifteen, I think. My wife and I had recently moved to Canterbury.'

'But, originally, I remember, you are from Atherstone, where my husband's family is from.' Addressing her husband, who was coming towards them from the window, she continued, 'Do you hear that, dear?'

'Hmm,' Sir Christopher again made his noise. 'Small world. Atherstone, as they say, is a good place to come *from*.'

'Exactly what the interviewer said to me when I got my first job in the Met,' Warne said to everybody, feeling some relief that he was at least back on court with Lady Penelope's bastard of a husband.

7

'That's one unhappy marriage,' Liz said, when they were back in the car.

'Publicly it isn't. But Sir C's screwed around.'

'And you've frolicked in their circle!'

'That dinner you mean. Nah. It was what the university calls a town-gown event, PR. I represented the local fuzz. Clarice was a teachers' rep. Before the port, cheese, and coffee were served, the gentlemen were asked to move several places to their left, and I found myself sitting next to Lady P.'

Who's a bastard now, he said to himself. You were pissed and made sure you sat next to her. You told that old buzzard, who should have had the seat, he hadn't counted right.

'Lady P's friendly, but on edge,' Liz said.

'I only noticed her friendliness. She insisted I call her Penelope, but absolutely not "Penny". She was pleased I knew about Atherstone, and the old village, Farmwell, which is part of her husband's name. It's more or less disappeared now, swallowed up by Manchester. I told her about Clarice and me, before we were married, walking past the family house on the outskirts of Atherstone, a big arts and crafts place. It used to be a bit run down, but a premiership footballer from the Ivory Coast lives in it now with his extended family. Everything's restored and more. He didn't want mock Tudor in Cheshire.'

'What brought Sir Christopher down here?'

'In 1949 he married Penelope Fincham, an heiress to the

Fincham farming and brewery fortune. People in Atherstone still say he was outraged by the Labour landslide in forty-five, a lot of stuff about "appalling ingratitude to Churchill, who'd saved our heritage and future." Also there was the nationalisation of coal. The Farmwell-Pemburys owned coal mines around Atherstone, though they'd never invested much in them. All but one of them was exhausted by the time they were nationalised. I guess Sir Christopher's always been more comfortable in Conservative Kent. Lady Penelope told me at the dinner that none of their friends in Kent knew anything about the North.'

Liz offering no response to this, Warne felt again the impact of Clarice's scorn all those years ago.

'What was it like flirting with Lady Penelope over the port and cheese?'

'Don't be daft, Clarice. She's as old as my mother. Different though. She delights in men's attention, and men want to please her. If there'd been a puddle in her way in that dining-hall, one of the old buffers would have spread his dinner-jacket over it for her to walk on.'

'He'd have had to shoulder-charge you out of the way first.'

'Come on, Clarice. You're having me on. I just kept feeding her lines. You can always have people like that on a lead, if you indulge them and laugh at their jokes.'

'Which means she had you on a lead. I hope you haven't forgotten that our great-grandparents and grandparents, and your mother, worked in her father-in-law's cotton mill, which he re-named Prospero's, as if he was inviting all the workers to live with him on an enchanted island. My grandma was deafened for life in one ear, when she was a scavenger working under an unguarded machine, and was struck by one of its moving parts. She got bugger-all in compensation from the Farmwell-Pemburys. She was fifteen! All her life her hair had to be cut awkwardly to conceal the scar.'

Now, in the car with Liz, Warne remembered Lady Penelope asking if he'd heard of Prospero's.

Guiltily he saw, as if he were looking at himself in a film, the fixed complicit smile on his face, as he poured more port into his glass, and replied, 'Who hasn't who comes from Atherstone?'

Clearly expecting him to be entertained by anecdotes which must have amused many a family gathering, Lady Penelope told how Sir Christopher's father had acquired the cotton mill, which became Prospero's, for 'next to nothing;' buying it from an old school friend, partly in return for loans to meet his 'tremendous gambling debts.'

Then came more; all the kerfuffle, long talked about in Atherstone, about what happened when the new name was painted on the factory chimney.

'When the workmen first painted the name up two sides of the chimney,' Lady Penelope said, 'they understandably forgot the apostrophe. They had to go back up the scaffolding to squeeze it in between the o and the s.'

'It was always a bit cramped,' he replied.

'According to my husband,' Lady Penelope went on, 'the workers could never do enough for his father. Some of them were almost his friends, especially when he gave them free tickets to see him on stage.'

Listening to these words at the dinner, Warne felt the rage emanating from Clarice, fifteen yards away, where she and Warne had originally been placed. Clarice's great-granddad was the workman sent back up the scaffolding.

'Prospero's made the family a great deal of money,' Lady Penelope concluded. 'Eventually it was sold at a huge profit before cheap imports began to destroy the Lancashire cotton industry and deprive poor workers, many of them recent immigrants from Pakistan, of their livelihood.'

'The chimney's down now,' Warne replied, but Lady Penelope had turned to the man on her other side.

Momentarily isolated from both the women alongside him, he remembered that Prospero's, along with an early eighteenth century Unitarian chapel, and the late nineteenth century town hall and library, was the most distinguished building in Atherstone. At one corner a dome you might have found on a church surmounted the internal staircase for workers to troop up and down, and dentil moulding separated the topmost windows from the flat roof. The main entrance was a courtyard, from which a double-sided curved staircase ascended to the offices, as if to the chambers of a Renaissance palace. Every day after leaving school at fourteen, his mother had walked up these steps as an office-girl, until her abrupt retirement, age nineteen, because of a sudden nervous breakdown. Reading Faulkner at university, he wondered if Mississippi slaves had picked cotton destined for the mill that became Prospero's. Later he saw that Clarice was right. Its name had been chosen to beguile and mock its workers, just as Southern slaves were given names from classical history and literature. No wonder Muhammad Ali renounced his slave name, 'Cassius Clay'.

'The offices were bearable enough,' his mother used to say of Prospero's, 'but on the factory floors it was hell on earth.'

No unions there, and none in the Farmwell-Pembury coal mines and nuts and bolts works.

Thinking Lady Penelope was turning back to him at the dinner, he announced, 'All sorts of firms are in Prospero's now: double-glazing, car parts, carpets.'

But she still ignored him.

That night, as Clarice and he prepared for bed, Clarice said to him, 'If I'd have sat next to Lady Penelope, I'd have asked her who Prospero's had in mind for Miranda and Caliban. You've seen photos of my grandma before the accident. She was as beautiful as any Miranda, but the Farmwell-Pemburys exploited her as Caliban. As for Sir Christopher's father fancying himself an actor, my grandma said he was just an old goat. Don't be alone with him!'

'You're as beautiful as any Miranda,' Warne responded, aware of how pathetic he sounded.

'Listen to yourself,' Clarice declared passionately. 'Don't get suckered in. I'll teach. You solve the crimes. But for God's sake let's not sell ourselves.'

I'm always trying not to, my love, Warne thought, as Liz now turned up the Old Dover Road and into the station.

At the dinner he hadn't mentioned to Lady Penelope that his mother was an office-girl training to be a secretary at Prospero's. This information might have led on to his mother's breakdown, and perhaps her eventual marriage to his dad, 'Flagger Bill', after that cunt of a trainee-solicitor she was engaged to asked for his ring back. It might also have led to the minimal medical treatment his mother received.

Atherstone didn't believe workers could suffer from psychological problems.

8

'Tough on crime; tough on the causes of crime,' Blair proclaimed.

Another meaningless soundbite, Warne reflected, as he waited for Vincent Clements to arrive.

How tough? Flog, cut off hands, balls, hang? Some law-abiding UK citizens would say yes to all of that, especially for paedophiles. Some coppers in the station were muttering Mark Farmwell-Pembury was asking for it.

Should they press for GBH for the assault on the American student?

Immediately after the attack Liz had arrested the three Rogers brothers; all unemployed, the two oldest, twenty and nineteen, members of the BNP, the youngest, sixteen, just tagging along.

'I guess my son's colour, his advantages and his accent must have got to them,' the father of the student said sorrowfully, sitting in Warne's office and expressing his admiration at the prompt arrest.

A black dentist in Boston he'd speedily arrived in Canterbury.

'We're Catholics,' he revealed, as if to explain his son's research project into the conversion of Britain to Christianity.

The project was why his son, arriving at Canterbury University after Christmas, had been given a special tour of St Augustine's Abbey in the city. Coming out of the abbey in the dusk, the young man had momentarily lost his way and asked the passing Rogers brothers for directions. Their response was to beat him up, stab him in the shoulder, and run away with his wallet and briefcase.

'Men like the Rogers brothers don't have much else to hold on to, apart from racism,' Liz said.

'You mean they've lost everything else, whatever that was?' the father replied. 'These poor devils are in my country too.'

'If I had a son,' Liz said, when she and Warne were alone, 'he might look very like the young man who's in hospital.'

Reaching the door, she turned back to declare, 'Race, you know, it's always there. You think it isn't, and you can relax, but it is; white people wishing you simply didn't exist, believing all their problems would disappear, if they could eliminate you from their world.'

Tough on racism, tough on the causes of racism, Warne thought, waiting for Vincent Clements; tough on stealing lead, tough on the causes of stealing lead; tough on bike theft, tough on the causes of bike theft. You could go on forever. At least the racket with the kids' bikes should be simple to solve.

A WPC knocked on his door and put her head around it.

'DS Ozeoke-Bruce says the prince has arrived,' she announced puzzled. 'She's bringing him to your office.'

No puzzle for him who the prince was. He'd been told by the manager of Clements Antiques, 'Vincent's a prince to work for; the most considerate employer anyone could have.'

But it was only when Vincent Clements was in his office that he understood more of what 'princeliness' might mean in this case. It seemed to clear a space around Vincent, as if nothing he touched, even in Warne's office, could ever soil him. Nearly sixty, and wearing a cream felt fedora, he was tall, tanned, weighty, and scented; his body assertively full of good eating and drinking, and swelling in a curve of his chest and stomach down to the belt of his trousers. Beneath his purple cashmere jacket his buttercup turtleneck shirt of very fine cotton was tucked smoothly into black trousers that rested, at his ankles, on the glowing punched leather of his tan brogues. Facing him, Warne felt he hadn't given enough thought to what he'd put on that morning. Liz too, he noticed, was tucking in her shirt and buttoning and unbuttoning her jacket.

'Thanks for coming,' he said, as he shook hands. 'Do sit down. How was Marrakech?'

'Diverting and restful, as always,' Vincent responded, removing his hat to reveal a shaven skull also exuding pleasure. 'I've had a house there for seventeen years. Do you know it?'

'I spent ten days there and in the Atlas mountains five years ago, with my wife. I remember especially the Square of the Dead at the end of the afternoon; snake-charmers, story-tellers, acrobats, fire-eaters; teeming with people; then the dramatic call to prayers.'

'The *Djemaa el-Fna*. I sat overlooking it last Saturday. You're right, so much life, just happening; like an immense theatre, performing whether you're there or not. I like its indifference to me. There's a comfort in not belonging to a place; accepting the surface, asking no questions, never being expected to do anything about anything; just fit in anonymously, obligations only to one's friends. Irresponsible of me, I know, but I have learned Arabic, and that's not easy.'

'Sandwich must seem sleepy, by contrast.'

'I can't stand the winters. But it's had its day, and the world's cameras come for the open golf championship, when I make a fortune renting my house. You know it used to be the most important naval base in England. It was burned by the French, twice, and four hundred years later they colonised Morocco. Before the French the Romans had their say in both places.' Turning to include Liz, he continued, 'Events choose their time and location for whatever happens, then move on. I try to stay out of the eye of any storm. I had enough turmoil in my adolescence.'

This was followed for a moment or two by silence. Warne felt as if they were actors, and one of them had forgotten the next line.

Liz cleared her throat, 'Talking about things moving on; there's stuff I need to do after this.'

Smiling and revealing Hollywood teeth, Vincent responded, 'You're anxious to hear about Mark.'

'It's why we're here,' Liz said.

Vincent paused, before announcing, '*mille e tre.*'

'What's that,' Liz exclaimed, a thousand and three, in Italian?'

'Yes, well done, Mozart's *Don Giovanni*,' Vincent responded. 'In the opera it's the number of women Don Giovanni's supposed to have had in Spain alone.'

'My wife and I saw *Don Giovanni* at English National Opera,' Warne said

'Mark saw the opera with me at Glyndebourne, one of the last things we ever did together. We were already on the verge of breaking up, because he was becoming a cruel predator. I seriously believe he saw a role model in the Don, and of course, in our modern age, he had no fear of hell's flames.'

'You're losing me,' Liz said.

Turning to her again, Vincent said, 'Mark lost interest in fidelity, said it was boring. I thought it meant I was boring, but then I realised it wouldn't make any difference who he was with, because Mark needed to hunt. Conquest obsessed him, especially over married men, or at least men with female partners, "so called straights", as he used to say.'

'So called straights,' Liz queried.

Vincent smiled at her. 'In his words, he liked to "turn them, convert them". He talked as if he were a master spy rousing the other side to the true cause, or a missionary converting infidels.'

'But where was his territory?' Warne asked.

All over, but often in the tied-pubs he looked after. There he had obvious power, especially over young landlords anxious to make a living. He could make or break them with a stroke of the pen, simply by changing their sales targets. He'd torment me with these exploits as we sat in his house in Chilham, which I'd helped him to transform, using my own architect and interior designer. He'd tell me how he would ask to see the pub cellar and, if he judged the moment right, put an arm around the man's shoulders, as if to comfort him. Next, there'd be a gentle kiss on the cheek accompanied by a roving hand. Some shoved him away. One smashed several of his teeth out. He said he'd fallen down the cellar steps. The dentistry cost him thousands. But others submitted. Mark told me it was as if they had been waiting for that moment all their lives. Later, there would be a night together in Mark's house, someone's flat, or a hotel.'

Vincent broke off, as a sad, tenseness flushed his face. Warne glimpsed the teeth again, wondering if Vincent and Mark had used the same dentist.

'Mark wasn't your pantomime, mincing gay,' Vincent continued. 'He was big, strong, brutal sometimes. You could be helpless. But he could also be so loving, and he was so handsome, beautiful. I've seen women fall for him at first sight.'

'Wasn't he worried about AIDS?' Warne asked.

'He had regular check-ups, and his male conquests, you know, were usually virgins, as far as other men were concerned. And Mark was always lucky, until the end of course.'

'You think his killer might be one of these publicans?' Liz asked.

'Possibly, but that's for you to find out. I'm just telling you about Mark.'

Letting this sink in, he then said, 'It wasn't just publicans, you know. There were the pick-ups at Dover, like the young man on the night Mark was killed, and there was the young man who killed himself, Paul Sewell, the son of the criminal.'

'What!' It was Warne's turn to exclaim.

'You didn't know, chief inspector! Dear me, another successful Farmwell-Pembury cover-up.'

'Mark had a relationship with Maurice Sewell's son?'

'Two or three years, off and on, till Mark ended it about the time the boy turned twenty. I'm told there were all sorts of hysterical scenes, when the boy simply wouldn't let go. He'd be drugged out of his mind and threatening to call in his father and have Mark cut up. You see, there was a lot of money involved, both ways. Mark's father had been borrowing money from the boy's father to cover debts run up at Aspinall's gambling clubs in London. Aspinall, you know, who has the zoos in Kent.'

'Howletts, Port Lympe,' Warne said, feeling he had to show he knew something.

'Exactly. But with Mark it was the other way round. The

boy would borrow large sums in cash from him, money from Farmwell-Pembury sources, always just for a few months, after which it would be returned also in cash, with interest for Mark to use as extra spending money. Mark, you know, was very extravagant. A new Aston Martin every two years didn't come cheap. There'd be fierce rows between him and Gillian, when she discovered temporary holes in the finances, though she knew nothing about the interest, or the rows would have been fiercer.'

Either way it's money-laundering, Warne thought, knowing Liz would be thinking the same thing. Sewell cleaning up his money through the F-Ps.

'I was glad Paul Sewell killed himself five years ago,' Vincent Clements continued, 'though by then it was long over between Mark and me.'

'Do you think Paul Sewell killed himself because of Mark?' Warne asked. 'Everybody said it was because he'd failed too many auditions.'

'Mark and he had been finished for several years, chief inspector, but again, that's for you to sort out. I'm telling you all this, but, believe me, I want to stay free of the Farmwell-Pemburys. I only wish now I'd never given Mark that paper knife.'

Silence, while sadness again penetrated Vincent's face. 'Mark's father,' he said, 'told me I disgusted him, and I was once arrested by the police only for being what I am. Till today I haven't been near a police station since.'

'I'm very sorry you were arrested,' Warne responded.

'The law!' Vincent replied ambivalently, standing up and gesturing theatrically to both Warne and Liz.

Thanking him, Warne accompanied him to his waiting taxi,

a Lexus LS 430, kept by a local firm for very special clients.

'Nora swishes me to and from the airports,' Vincent said, as she stood with the rear door open and made sure he was comfortably settled inside with the seatbelt fastened. Then she slid behind the wheel, easing the car powerfully and silently into the traffic and on to Sandwich.

'Can of worms,' Warne said to Liz, back in his office

'We're both thinking money-laundering.'

'Yeah.'

'So where do we go with it?'

'Dunno. Mark's dead. Paul Sewell's dead. Maurice Sewell's in jail partly for money-laundering, but with no mention of the F-Ps.'

'How were they kept out of it? We could question Sewell about the F-Ps.'

'Sir Christopher would deny everything we've just got from Vincent, and I can't see Vincent performing in a court. It would look like we're just fishing around, because we're getting nowhere with Mark's murder. Cunningham says I'm making a bloody fool of myself wanting Sir Christopher's and Lady Penelope's DNA.'

'We need it. We've identified as much DNA as we've found at Mark's house, except what must be theirs. Why can't we take a swab from them to be certain?'

'Sir Christopher won't have it, and Cunningham's backing him up.'

'F-P influence; money and power, just like Nigeria. Why do these people think they're so superior?'

'Because they've always been treated as superior.'

'But they've mixed with gangsters, killers. Suppose Maurice

Sewell had Mark killed, because Mark broke off with his son,' Liz said.

'Time-scale doesn't work. According to Vincent, Mark breaks off with Paul, when Paul's about twenty. That's fifteen years ago. Then Paul throws himself under a train in 1998, when he's thirty. Sewell wouldn't have waited till now, five years later, to have Mark killed, if he thought Mark was responsible for his son's death. If somebody actually was responsible, he'll already have dealt with it.'

'He doesn't wait long,' he left unsaid, knowing Liz was thinking it and thinking of Clarice.

After a couple of minutes Liz said, 'So we carry on searching for someone with a key to Mark's house, someone whose DNA trace we haven't found there among all the traces we have found.'

When he didn't answer, she continued, 'Sir Christopher's borrowed money from Sewell. His son's in bed with Sewell's son and is changing money with him. Sir Christopher doesn't want his DNA on record. I bet there's more here than our murder. Connections we're not getting to. I think there's more between the F-Ps and Sewell. You do too.'

And he was also beginning to wonder about Cunningham.

9

Ah, love, let us be true
To one another! For the world which seems
To lie before us like a land of dreams,
So various, so beautiful, so new,
Hath really neither joy, nor love, nor light,
Nor certitude, nor peace, nor help for pain;
And we are here as on a darkling plain;
Swept with confused alarms of struggle and flight,
Where ignorant armies clash by night.

Hand-written in pencil on a sheet torn from a school exercise book, as if they existed only between Peter Burgess and herself, these words had lived in Lady Farmwell-Pembury's heart since August 1940, when she was simply Penelope Fincham. But now, sleeplessly reviewing her life after the visit of the two detectives, she doubted if they could ever again console her. Mark's death re-opened too much reality; exposed again Gillian's unhappy marriage; confirmed Sir Christopher and Lady Farmwell-Pembury were no more than a performance.

Always she knew she had never again been as in love as she was with Peter in the spring and summer of 1939; Peter in his first season with Kent County Cricket Club; intending to go up to Oxford to read PPE, when he was twenty.

Urging her to, 'Go to university yourself. Read English literature or History. Someday, you know, I'm going to open the batting for England with Len Hutton.'

In June at Canterbury's St Lawrence cricket ground, with the great nineteenth century lime tree growing in the playing area, she watched him through her binoculars; seeing him inch his head in his cap to one side, as the ball reared frighteningly past his skull.

'Don't worry.' he assured her, at the end of the day's play, 'I've been blessed with very sharp eyes. Once I've read the wicket, I see what the ball's going to do, as soon as it leaves the bowler's hand.'

They were in his green MG Roadster, with the top down, driving her home to her parents' house, eight miles away in the village of Barham. His left hand squeezing her right, he promised, 'There's so much life before us.'

And so much poetry, 'Because no-one can say anything better than the great poets.'

Suddenly announcing, while they were eating their picnic lunch during a walk at the end of July in the beautiful Elham valley, 'I'd love to wake up with you.' Then, taking a slim book from his rucksack and reading, '*I wonder by my troth, what thou and I / Did, till we lov'd?*'; only telling her the poem was John Donne's *The Good-Morrow*, when he finished it.

'Poems like that would have been too exciting for my girls boarding school,' she responded, as he moved to kiss her, her whole being opening to him, when he said, 'I want to love you, marry you, and sleep with you.'

Then the next words, foreboding even now in her bed at Nystole.

'We may be running out of world enough and time, as another poet says. There's going to be a war. I'm going to volunteer.'

His reasons prepared.

'My history teacher, Mr Rosenbloom, says life is unbearable for his relatives and friends in Germany. They're being disbarred from their professions. Husbands and fathers are dragged from their offices and beaten in the streets by mobs. Synagogues have been ransacked and destroyed. Things like this happened to the de Burgeois, my Huguenot ancestors in seventeenth century France. It's why they fled to Canterbury. We mustn't let history repeat itself.'

War or no war, she would have agreed to the weekend in that country pub near Lewes in Sussex. In her bed now, she whispered to herself: '*Busie old foole, unruly Sunne,/ Why dost thou thus,/ Through windows, and through curtains call on us?/ Must to thy motions lovers seasons run?*'. More lines from John Donne she'd discovered especially for Peter, murmuring them to him, as they both woke that first morning, getting no further into the poem, before he rolled on top of her, sighing blissfully, when she wrapped herself around him.

Breakfast in their room, her best meal ever, and almost her last with Peter, because he was dead within a few months, killed at Dunkirk in May 1940, as part of the British Expeditionary Force.

No body to bury, so no grave for her broken heart to weep over. Dug in, protecting the retreat, his position was directly hit by a shell.

Had those sharp eyes seen it coming, she wondered uselessly for years? Had Peter known there would be no swaying any part of himself out of its way?

Only the pathetically small parcel of his personal possessions surviving and arriving at his parents' house in August; among them an unsealed envelope with her name written on the front and the lines from Matthew Arnold's *Dover Beach* inside.

Lines she had read at school.

But with no idea then of the ultimate horror amid which her own lover would need to share their passionate appeal.

No idea of the nightmares of the wounded and dying she would be called on to soothe as an auxiliary nurse.

True to one another?

What could that mean, when Peter was dead?

Never to marry?

To marry, but always remember?

Preserve a surface, and always remember?

A land of dreams amid the heartache.

A lady to her knight, even before he was a knight.

'You can't be Christopher's wife and expect him to live with the ghost of Peter,' her younger sister Judith said. 'Mind you, I'm not sure I trust Christopher an inch.'

Meeting Christopher at one of the parties in London after the war. Just over six feet, like Peter, his hair well-combed and blond; Peter's dark brown and unruly. A very handsome hero. If she didn't marry him, any one of the women clustering around him in supplication certainly would.

Battle-hardened throughout North Africa and Italy.

'Not a scratch on me.'

A strong man to share the burden of grief.

'All the British working man needs is a firm hand, a firm lead, but not from these damned Socialists, who might as well be Communists.'

He was taking her on a tour of the industries his family owned in and around Atherstone.

What about the British working woman?

Her first ever political thought. Hardly any since.

The women she'd driven ambulances with?

The working women she saw in FARMWELL-PEMBURY NUTS & BOLTS, one of the several concerns the family owned in Atherstone?

Left with the manager, while Christopher was called to the telephone; asking to look inside the works.

Snap-time; women in their overalls at a table; hands and fingers gripping their mugs and sandwiches horribly scarred and disfigured, as if subjected to unspeakable torture. How could you make love, or soothe a child, with hands so maimed?

The manager blandly explaining, 'The nuts and bolts are very rough and sharp-edged. These women are sorting them with their bare hands nine hours a day.'

Christopher fiercely rebuking him, 'I told you she was not allowed inside that hell-hole.'

Under pressure to marry him.

Her father declaring, soon after Christopher was introduced to the family, 'We haven't brought you up to become an old maid, Penelope. Hundreds of girls not nearly as attractive as you have lost fiancés; thousands of wives have lost husbands. I'm sure Peter would not expect you never to accept another man. I think Christopher and he might have been friends. Christopher will bring new energy to the Fincham future.'

But he will never read poetry to me, she thought, and if he were batting, and knew he'd edged the catch to slip, he would never walk back to the pavilion before the umpire's decision.

Mrs Thatcher knighting him, then offering him a peerage.

Turning the peerage down. That famous television interview, 'When I want to slumber on leather upholstery, I'll do so in my own house in Kent.'

Another of his lies.

But what was the truth?

Challenge him, he glazed over.

Vulnerability was for other people.

He and his friends imprisoning her in adulation like a virgin in a fairy tale.

'Christopher's a lucky man!'

'I wanted to marry you, as soon as I saw you at that party in London. None of the other girls stood a chance.'

Allowance for her sorrow over Peter, because give someone an allowance, you can have them where you want them.

DS Ezeoke-Bruce in the library this afternoon too independent a woman for him; putting her Nigerian name first; too much respect paid to her by the chief inspector.

The closest she'd ever sat to someone who was not white; closer than she'd been to Enoch Powell MP, when he sat next to her at her dinner-table nearly forty years ago, and rehearsed his anti-immigration 'rivers of blood' speech to everyone present, telling them that, because of immigration, 'the black man would soon hold the whip hand over the white man.'

All weekend his insufferable vanity; his cruel reasoning driving himself as near to the verge of madness, as it was driving her.

Christopher fully supporting him.

Playing the accommodating wife and mother, dutifully attending to all her guests' needs.

Always true to the system she was in; wearing its clothes.

Never daring to break through any surface, descend ever again into any horror.

Unlike Judith, who came to the dinner, with her then husband, from their house in Rye.

'I wouldn't open my doors to Enoch Powell if he were wandering lost and naked on Romney Marsh in freezing wind and rain. It's about time you stood up to Christopher wrapping himself in the flag. Where's he going to stick the flagpole? The ground's shifting under all our feet. It's not coloured red any more, except by blood from wars being fought all over the world. And why have you been sent to stay with me now? Is it true what your driver hinted to me, that military people are secretly meeting at Nystole? Is Christopher losing his mind? To overthrow a Labour government, or any government, is treasonable. Why don't you even drive yourself anymore? You're not the queen!'

Judith bringing Mark back into the family-fold, ten years after Christopher denounced him when he was nineteen; Christopher letting Judith dominate the gathering, because he was still distracted by a mysterious business trip he'd recently taken to the Bahamas on behalf of the government.

'Mark likes sex with a man,' Judith declared. 'I like sex with a man. Where's the problem?'

Judith having an affair with the architect, Jack Donaldson, who asked ordinary people what kind of houses they would like before he designed them.

'That architect chappie,' Christopher said, until Tony Blair became prime minister, and he was, 'that architect chappie, who's just been knighted by this Labour government, along with all those honours to entertainment people.'

Judith protesting to her, fifteen years ago, 'Break everything up. Christopher can look after himself. Nobody knows where he is half the time. There's money enough for everybody, and the firm doesn't matter. What matters is your life, the only one you'll ever have. Decade after decade you've indulged yourself in sorrow. It's a conceit, an illness. You're a bad example to Gillian, who's martyring herself keeping the firm on the road. She's another who should have dumped her husband years ago. From the word go he's been a womaniser, who only married her to further his family's wine business. I know I haven't kept my marriage vows, but it's only been with Jack Donaldson, and we're as in love with each other as any Darby and Joan.'

'We should padlock your sister's mouth,' Christopher said.

DS Ezeoke-Bruce's card lay on her bedside table. If she phoned the detective, how much would she have to reveal?

10

'So you're the one who knocked Mark Farmwell-Pembury's teeth out.'

'Fucking queer, I'd do it again; me and my wife working our arses off behind the bar; pub full of lunchtime trade, and he swans in demanding to see the cellar. Anything he got he was asking for it.'

'Asking to be killed?'

'If a fucking pervert ever touched any one of my sons ...'

What? What would you do?

Sleepless all night, the exchange with the publican and the final, unasked question incessantly re-played themselves in Warne's tortured mind.

What would you do that I'd have to clear up?

Why was he still wading in all this shit? Why had he involved Clarice in it? She only wanted to be a teacher. He could have been a teacher himself. Still could be.

Wrap Farmwell-Pembury up. Prove Sewell killed Clarice. I'm out.

No more spending all day interviewing publicans Mark Farmwell-Pembury might have fucked; refusing pints; Liz and three DCs tackling their list.

That last one in Wye. The night Mark was killed, he was at the hospital in Ashford, sleeping in a chair at the side of his youngest son's bed.

Burly, violent, tattooed, protective, dad.

He'd have pulled the bike over, got off and challenged the Mondeo driver.

'What's your fucking game?'

Assuming the Mondeo driver hadn't driven straight over him. Desolate nights in bed.

Already, a whole year since Clarice was murdered.

Was he supposed simply to get used to it, like all the other widowers and widow; bereaved parents; everyone eventually death's victim?

Out of the house by six, walking down the Whitstable Road, around the Roman Westgate and, passing through a city centre disturbed only by early delivery vans, at his desk in thirty minutes.

Budgets and rosters sorted out, he took a break. Sitting with his legs resting across a corner of the desk, he skimmed through *The Guardian*. Needing simple pleasure, he turned purposefully to the sports section: Newcastle 2 United 6; Scholes hat-trick, United top of the Premiership. Better than the day of the demo, United nil, Arsenal 2, United out of the cup.

Better still the 1998-99 treble season: 2-1 against Arsenal in the cup semi-final at Villa Park, Giggs's wonder goal. And, against Arsenal again, another 2-1 victory in January 1970, Willie Morgan scoring the winner, a game he never forgot, because it was his first visit to Old Trafford with his dad, thirty odd years ago; travelling the nine miles from Atherstone on the back of his dad's 500cc Triumph, a descendant of Brando's bike in *The Wild One*, its power surging through his eight year old body. Even when it was parked in the garage, his mother would never sit on it. As soon as it was dusk, she switched a light on in every room and locked the front and back doors.

'I'm worried stiff, when you set off on that motor bike, Bill,' she said, 'and now you're taking David with you. What if I lost you both? You could go in the car.'

'More fun on t' bike, Jeaney, love. Easier parkin'. Quicker gerrin away. Don't frighten yourself. You know, I'll always look after all of us.'

Dead both of them now, like Clarice and her mum and dad, and like thousands already killed in Iraq. Warne knew he'd no idea what sense death made, meaning he'd no idea what sense life made, especially when life became a machine for producing death. Overwhelming western fire-power had captured Baghdad. Saddam's statue had been toppled by triumphant American troops first placing the Stars and Stripes over its face, then putting a chain noose around its neck and attaching the chain to a winding mechanism on an armoured truck. On TV he'd seen the statue break at the knees and slowly crash down into a scrum of people, who began to beat it with shoes and sticks.

'Loaded with symbolism,' the commentators said; but of what? Suppose the victory, if it was a victory, was as hollow as the statue? Before the invasion he'd heard a retired American general declaring it would take several hundred thousand soldiers both to win a war with Iraq, and then to maintain control of the country.

Liz came into his office, just as he was thinking about Mark Farmwell-Pembury and homosexuality in Saddam's Iraq. She looked shaken. In her hand was an A4 envelope.

'We've got nowhere with Mark and pub landlords,' she said immediately, as if to settle herself.

'Me neither.'

'All we've done is embarrass a few, who've settled back down with their wives or female partners. Two of them have already come out, left the pubs they were in and found male partners. They've all got good stories about where they were the night Mark was killed, and it wasn't in that wet-room.'

'Cunningham and Maidstone can't believe we're stymied,' he responded, 'though I don't admit that. And an unsolved mystery suits the F-P publicity people. It means they can do what they like with it; keep prying eyes away from Mark's life, while making side-swipes at us. You've seen they're blaming us for not stopping people on the streets drinking beer from cans and bottles. Street drinking's a pain, I know, but the F-Ps want to hamstring the supermarket drinks trade.'

'So what do we do? Nothing's coming in from our usual sources; no leads, no rumours. Do we just wait for something to turn up?'

'Tell me what else, Liz.'

'The killer was at Mark's birthday party on the Saturday night, I'm sure. That's where all the DNA's from, apart from the cleaner's. We've gotta break one of their alibis.'

When he didn't reply, she took an A4 black and white photograph from the envelope in her hand. Placing it face-up on his desk, she said, 'This is a copy of what was waiting for me, when I got home last night. It came through the post, London post-mark. The original and the envelope are already with forensics.'

He looked at a photograph he remembered seeing first, twenty-odd years ago, when he was a student writing about Faulkner. Jesus, no wonder Liz was on edge. The photograph was of a nineteenth century illustration of a scene on the main deck of a ship transporting slaves to the States. In the scene a female slave was hanging naked, upside down, from a rope tied to her left ankle. Necessarily, her right leg splayed away from her left exposing her genitalia to a leering white man.

'Jesus,' he repeated, out loud.

'Somebody doesn't like me arresting the Rogers brothers,' Liz said.

'The bastards will have a hard time denying a racial motive for the attack on the student after this,' he responded angrily.

Taking the photo back, Liz reached his office door, as he said, 'You're still good for promotion, Liz. Don't be set back by this.'

He meant it. Liz was full of initiative. She'd had half a dozen kids, whose bikes had been stolen in Stoke Newington, brought to the barn in Pett Bottom, where they'd identified their own bikes among the bikes for sale. Crime solved. Lead, though, was still disappearing from church roofs in Kent, and now computers were being stolen from the university; dopey academics leaving ground floor office windows open all night.

Towards noon a uniform he didn't know knocked on the door and bobbed his head into the room.

'Woman to see you.'

'Woman? Who?'

'She says you'll know her as Jane Scott, from Atherstone.'

'Jane Scott!'

He knew a Jane Scott from Atherstone all right, but why was she in Canterbury? She and Clarice and he had been at school together, and she'd come to Canterbury for Clarice's funeral. When they were all seventeen, Jane Scott, blond and nearly as sexy as her older sister, Marilyn, had asked him if he always wanted to be with Clarice. When he said, 'Yes,' she'd gone on to fail all her A levels, get herself pregnant with a plumber, and live with him for about a year after the birth of a daughter. Since that relationship ended, she'd brought up her daughter as a single mother and become a successful business woman in the plumbing trade. She'd bought a house in the vicinity of what was known as 'millionaires' row' in Worsley, about eight miles from Manchester. Ryan Giggs lived in the same locality.

11

'So it's *the* Jane Scott!'

'Hello, David; or should I still say "Chief Inspector David Warne"?'

'I'm always David to anyone who knows me from Atherstone.'

The awestruck PC had brought her to his office. When he left, they briefly kissed, cheek to cheek, each holding the shoulder of the other.

'You'll be surprised to see me,' Jane began.

'Surprised doesn't say half of it.'

She never changes much, he thought, sitting behind his desk; gym-fit, blond hair still fabulous, like her older sister Marilyn's and their mother's. No wonder testosterone was pumping through that young PC. He remembered her mother had served in Atherstone's best bread and cake shop. Walking past it in the morning on the way to school, you got a wonderful smell of newly baked bread, and meat and potato pies. Her father was a dutiful, bald-headed, postman.

'You're surviving?' Jane asked. She obviously had Clarice in mind.

'Surviving's about right.'

'Clarice and you never deserved what happened to you both.'

'Deserving doesn't have much to do with most things.'

'Not in your case, that's for sure.'

They were silent, as he observed her well cut trouser suit, which was of a slightly lighter blue than the expensive coat he'd helped her to take off, releasing her musky perfume, especially when she shook out her hair.

'Can I get you a drink of something?' he asked. 'Tea, coffee, water? Only the water will be any good. Or we could go for lunch, somewhere.'

'I don't need anything now, but lunch would be nice. I'm getting an afternoon train back to Manchester. I came down to the County Hotel yesterday, and I've come here straight from an interview with Professor Howard Willetts at Canterbury University. I know I should have made an appointment with you, but I hadn't intended to bother you. You must be very busy. I saw you on TV news about the Farmwell-Pembury murder case, and the local paper at the hotel was full of it. It's just that Professor Willetts wasn't at all helpful, though I understand his point about confidentiality.'

'You can always come and see me any time, and I know Howard Willetts. He's in English. I met him originally through Clarice. She ran a liaison group between local schools and the university's English department. Howard's actually a friend. What did you want from him?'

'I'm trying to find Marilyn's daughter.'

'Marilyn's daughter! I didn't know she had a daughter.'

'Not many people did. When the daughter was born, Marilyn was twenty-three and living in London.'

'She brought the daughter up herself in London?'

'Not really, once the child could go to a nursery. I'm sure she thought the father would marry her, and I don't know why he didn't. Whoever he was nobody knows. He paid for an expensive maternity hospital in Surrey, nursery schools, boarding school; financed his daughter right through university. Marina, that's the daughter, never really needed our side of the family. My mum and dad wouldn't have been much help in the circles she moved in, even if she'd asked them, and I was too busy sorting out my own life and my business. We all just thought, well, at least she's not short of money.'

'Marina,' Warne said. 'That's Shakespeare, one of the last plays.'

'I don't know where the name's from.'

'Marina Scott?'

'Yes, she had to be Marina something.'

'Sure. But where's Marilyn in all this? Why doesn't she find her daughter herself, if somebody has to?'

'Marilyn's dead, nearly two months ago.'

'Dead! How?'

'Cancer, right through her. Started in her breasts. Double mastectomy couldn't stop it.'

'Wow! Poor Marilyn.'

Cancer lurking in her lovely breasts, he thought, even if she'd been a Mother Theresa. Talk about deserving. Marilyn's breasts had pushed springily against him when he was sixteen and had dared to kiss her at a Valentine's party at her parents' house, just as he was arriving, and she was leaving for what must have been a less innocent scene. 'I'm too experienced for you, David,' she whispered, maybe sadly.

'There's money waiting for Marina and a penthouse in Manchester,' Jane continued, breaking the brief silence.

'Oh, yeah, I remember Marilyn went back North just as Clarice and me moved here to Canterbury.'

She serviced Maurice Sewell in London after his first wife's death, he recollected, though he doubted if Sewell was Marina's father. Joe Pawsey would know for sure.

'I lost track of her after she moved North,' he went on. 'A penthouse in Manchester! That must have cost a bomb.'

'A Saudi government official bought it for her, just after he took her to Bermuda.'

'She must have given him a helluva good time!'

'If you say so.'

'Sorry,' he said quickly. Then, after a moment or two, 'Let's get back to Marina. You still haven't told me what her connection is down here.'

'Marina was at Canterbury University. She graduated in 1997 with a first class degree in English and apparently disappeared soon afterwards. The Salvation Army can't trace her. No-one can. Professor Willetts admits she had a boy-friend, also in English, but won't tell me who he was.'

'I suppose she's not officially missing, not reported as missing.'

'She's missing for me, and I want to hand the money and property over to her.'

Typical of Jane, he thought; always looking out for others, generous and hospitable, like her parents; must be hard-headed, though, to run that business. What is it called? Pendlebury Plumbers, that's it. Never heard that she had another lasting relationship with a man. Wonder why not.

'There are always children who want to forget even perfectly good parents,' he said. 'Suppose Marina's working her way around the world. She could be anywhere. Suppose she's in Marilyn's business. It's not impossible.'

'I don't think so. She was twenty when I last saw her. She was the sort of person who'd want to stay immune, above it all, even superior.'

Bloody difficult if she looked anything like her mother and you, he thought.

By the time he was at university he knew for sure Marilyn was on the game, first in Manchester, next in London, though he understood it was always, from the beginning at the luxurious end of the market. She never stood half naked and hooked on drugs on wasted street corners, desperately inviting the kind of couplings he'd had to disturb in his days in the Met, when outraged residents regularly demanded a clean-up of their locality. Then he would bang on cars windows with his torch, making contorted twosomes and threesomes untangle, before sending some of the frustrated punters home to kiss wives and children. 'Escort girl' was the term some in Atherstone used, knowingly, of Marilyn. Others dug into what they remembered about Christine Keeler and Profumo.

Liz knocked on the door and put her head around it.

'See you a minute?' she asked.

'Who do we have here?' she said, nodding at the closed door, when he joined her in the corridor.

'Maybe a missing person.'

'For you to deal with!'

'I'll explain later. What do you have?'

'Caroline Edmondson's just been in. You know, the daughter of Gillian and Ralph, who are now in New Zealand.'

'And?'

'She's a bit worried her mother's making no contact. Phone and email, it's always her father. Caroline, or "Call Cal" as she's known on local radio, says this is very unusual, because she's much closer to her mother. Her father says her mother's gone on a tour of Australia, wild outback and everything.

Apparently, Caroline's dying New Zealand grandfather is hanging on and on.'

'Can we do anything with this?'

'Dunno.'

'At the other end of the world, why shouldn't Gillian break out of her shell, even forget her daughter for a bit? If anybody needs another life, she does.'

'So we just bear it in mind?'

'What else can we do?'

Liz made no response.

'Changing the subject,' Warne said, 'the woman in the interview room's a Jane Scott, from Atherstone, you know, my home town. Unofficially, she needs some help. I'm going to see what I can do, in my own time. First of all, I'm going to take her for lunch, before she catches a train for Manchester.'

'I might make a call to New Zealand,' Liz said. 'If I can get the time right.'

'No problem, 'Warne said. 'But won't it be midnight there now?'

12

On the way to lunch he walked with Jane into the underpass at the Riding Gate Roundabout. Leaning against one of the walls and expertly exploiting the underpass's echo chamber, a busker with a guitar was singing Dylan's *Lay, Lady, Lay*:

'Why wait any longer for the one you love, / When he's standing in front of you?'

So much passion in his voice; he might actually have been in his bedroom with his woman before him.

Pausing and searching into her handbag for her purse, Jane dropped a couple of pound coins into the busker's cap on the floor. Sensing tears in his eyes, Warne moved on ahead, waiting for Jane at the end of the underpass.

'Can we go to a pub?' She asked, catching up with him and looking a little bewildered by his moving on.

'That's easy,' he replied, sure his eyes were dry. 'The Dane John Gardens are here on the left. We can walk through them to The White Hart. In summer the gardens can be as crowded as Blackpool beach.'

At The White Hart they each had a chicken salad and a glass of white wine.

'I'd love to share a bottle with you,' Warne said, but I'm still in the middle of a working day.'

He was aware of a couple of older, solitary, men in the pub, nursing their pints, feasting their eyes on Jane, and thinking lucky bugger. Since Clarice's death, he'd never actually been alone in another woman's company, except with Liz at work. When would he have sex with a woman again? Who would she be? Frustration was driving him crazy. Grief couldn't repress it. Out of the blue here was Jane, knowing about him; next best thing to Clarice.

'Tell me about Pendlebury Plumbers,' he said.

'You really want to know?' she smiled, sipping her wine, and looking directly at him.

'Well, seeing you now, I wouldn't associate you with plumbing, but it must be a big part of your life.'

Signalling to the bar for a top-up, she sat back, saying provocatively, 'Running nipples, hexagon nipples, black strap-on boss, and I'm not talking "Carry On Plumbing".'

Laughing with pleasure for the first time for ages, he asked, 'What are you talking?'

'Pendlebury Plumbers is the biggest plumbing enterprise in the Manchester area.'

Letting this sink in, she continued, 'One thing my man left me with, apart from Fiona, my beautiful daughter, was knowing that plumbers can be hopeless at organising themselves. So, I began to do it for them, book all their appointments, order all the gear they required, invoice their customers, get the money in. Now, I employ a squad of twenty-five and have a supply store that keeps up with everything they need. It turns out I've a flare for business. Fiona, you know, went to Leeds like you, but she's a civil engineer. She's living in Paris. Her company sends her all over Europe.'

'Congratulations!' He lifted his glass to hers, 'I'm so happy for you.'

How could he not be, knowing what a wretched state she'd

been in, when Clarice and he left Atherstone for university; failing all her A levels in English, History, and Drama, and becoming pregnant?

'But what about you, on TV, arresting that big criminal, and now with the Farmwell-Pemburys!' Sipping more wine, she said, 'My mother worked at Prospero's before she moved to the cake shop, and my grandma was a cleaner at their house. Every year they gave a Christmas dinner for their house staff. They cooked it and waited on the tables themselves, like the royal family at one of their castles. My grandma said you had to keep a look-out for Charles Farmwell-Pembury, Sir Christopher's father. He had wandering palms; thought they had a right to wander up your skirt.'

'Sir Christopher screws around down here, but there's been no complaints, so far. Our grandparents, Clarice's and mine, worked at Prospero's, and you know my mother worked in the offices for a few years, until she had her breakdown. Clarice's great-granddad was one of the mill's maintenance men. He was sent up the scaffolding to paint Prospero's on the chimney.'

'The lettering never looked quite right,' Jane commented, smiling and finishing her wine.

As she said this, he heard Clarice's contempt in his ear, 'Risking great-granddad's life, twice, up that scaffolding! Just to satisfy Farmwell-Pembury vanity.'

Disconcertingly, he found himself comparing Clarice and Jane. He remembered his mother, always glad of reassurance, liked the openness and friendliness of Jane's smile, when she used to come to the house in her teens, and liked discussing clothes with her. His mother was an expert dress-maker, and her skills fascinated Jane, though the two women had very different tastes, his mother's style always being restrained, and always, therefore, appealing to Clarice, who had no time for women 'flopping their boobs about.' His mother hardly ever discussed clothes with Clarice, but when he was eighteen it had suddenly struck him, that if his mother could have been any other woman on earth, it would have been a young Clarice Wellman going to Oxford University.

They had their coffee, and he signalled for the bill, which he insisted on paying. Then they walked to the County Hotel, whose gloomy oak interior always seemed to Warne to be awaiting an Agatha Christie murder. After collecting Jane's suitcase, he pulled it on its wheels to the West Station.

'Back to the grind for us both,' Jane said, as they stood on the platform.

'I'll see what I can find out about Marilyn's daughter in my spare time,' he responded. 'Howard Willetts will tell me anything he knows.'

'Do you have spare time?'

Seeing the train approach, they kissed cheek to cheek, hugging each other so closely, he was taken back again to his Valentine's kiss with Marilyn. Then, as they stood slightly apart, still holding each other's arms, he saw there were now tears in Jane's eyes.

Looking at him through the tears, she said, 'Until today I haven't been so close to you since that moment when we were both seventeen, and I asked you if you always wanted to be with Clarice. I'm a mature business-woman now, a single-mother with a grown-up, independent daughter. But my feelings for you have never changed, and I want to tell you now, because I'll be sorry if I don't, and I may never get another chance. You are still the love of my life, always have been.'

Leaving him with a sudden feeling of nearly overwhelming loneliness, she pulled her suitcase into the nearest carriage, its door closing behind her.

'You're the love of my life.'

Words he said to Clarice, as they both prepared for their different universities.

'Don't you think it's a bit early for that?' she replied.

13

Later that day he sat in the re-assuringly calm office of Professor Howard Willett's secretary. He'd phoned to fix up a meeting for four-thirty, but Howard still had someone with him.

'Tea, coffee, anything but alcohol?' the secretary asked, showing him to a comfortable easy chair near a coffee table, on which an array of university and English department publicity was fanned out.

'I'm O.K. Thanks. I'll just sit and wait.'

'You are still the love of my life, always have been.'

How brave of Jane to say these words after all those years; expose herself to him again; risk rejection again.

Instantly, on the station platform, he knew there was no chance he'd reject her.

Other possible loves must always exist. Clarice knew that. It's what her reply to him meant, when they were eighteen, even though, knowing Jane wanted him, she also said at that time, 'I couldn't bear to see you with another girl.'

He never doubted her fidelity, though he strayed himself, once at university; hardly even a one night stand; that woman bi-sexual banker using him for a thirty minute shag.

Clarice and Jane loving him. How lucky could a man be?

A tall, solidly formed woman, about thirty-five came out of Howard's office, looking determined.

Howard followed, looking bothered.

'David, buddy,' he said, extending his hand. 'Come in.'

Entering Howard's spacious, book-lined office, an oasis of tranquillity in any world-setting, he made for his usual restful chair.

'That was Liesbeth van Noortwijk,' Howard announced, 'the new Director of Student Experience.'

'Yeah?'

'Her family's Dutch, though they've long been settled in England, and she has a Scottish partner. As soon as she came in, she more or less kneed me in my puny academic nuts by telling me she cycled two hundred miles over the weekend. Then, while I was still squirming, she announced I'm facing a complaint from two women students. Can you believe it? First from Warwick, Masters and Ph.D. from Yale, nearly thirty years teaching, and someone with a sports science degree and working towards a Ph.D. in management systems, comes into my office and tells me these women have reported my behaviour to be sexist.'

'Shall I put you under caution?'

Flopping into his tan, high back, all leather, padded swivel chair behind his desk, Howard looked alarmed, then blew air out of his lips and smiled.

'Ah, buddy,' he said. 'All I've done is suggest to two women students they were inappropriately dressed.'

'Yeah?'

'Boobs, bras, thongs, nearly naked, I'm not kidding, all winter; sitting one on each side of me at a seminar table, week after week. Sexual intimidation! All I take into a room when I teach is a pencil, the text, and the class-list. In one seminar I nearly stuck my pencil into the cleavage of one of the women, while I searched for a quotation from *Paradise Lost*!'

And all I'm dealing with is my wife murdered and a gay man stabbed to death in his own wet room.

'I should have done music, like my poor old dad wanted me to,' Howard said. It was a version of a refrain Warne and Clarice had heard at various times for more than a decade.

Early in their friendship Howard had told them of his terrible teenage rows about jazz with his father, head of music at a high-powered school in Gloucestershire; how his father wanted him to go to the Royal Academy as a first study pianist; how, with a pair of garden secateurs, his father had cut up an Oscar Peterson LP right in front of his sixteen years old face, while he was trying to watch *Dr Who* on TV; how, in vain revenge, he spurned the Royal Academy and decided on English at Warwick.

'Anyway, let's move on,' Howard said. 'You tell me you want to talk about Marina Scott, who graduated in 1997.'

'Yeah. It's not official police business, you understand. I'm just trying to help a friend, Jane Scott. You saw her this morning. She came to see me afterwards. She came to Clarice's funeral.'

'I'm surprised I missed her there. But how do you know her? She never mentioned you.'

'She didn't intend to get me involved, but didn't know where else to turn, after she'd seen you. She went to the same school as Clarice and me.'

'Atherstone again, your inescapable past! You'll never get away from it.'

'Seems so.'

'Not that anyone would ever have wanted to get away from Clarice.' He paused, and then said, 'I'll always miss her, and

Cindy misses her too; not as much as you must miss her, but there we are. I still hear her lovely alto voice, and I loved playing the piano with her. She kept the faith, in teaching literature, I mean, among all the slipping and sliding. You know, King Lear or Coronation Street? We've cultural studies people here who give them equal status. And the same actors will do either, if the money's right.'

Aunty Lucy arrived in Warne's head, when Howard mentioned Coronation Street. Still a force, though crippled by angina, she saw the first three or four episodes of Coronation Street in black and white, then never watched the programme again, because she immediately judged it to be 'an insult to the working class.'

'I've always appreciated your respect for Clarice.'

Well before Cindy Robinson lived with Howard, he'd once told Clarice he thought Howard fancied her. It was just after he'd watched them sitting closely together at Howard's Steinway, playing Mendelssohn's *Overture to a Midsummer Night's Dream*, arranged for four hands, Howard, closing his eyes as the piece ended and, his fingers resting on the keys, turning passionately to his left to kiss her cheek.

'He'd have been all over you, if I hadn't been there.'

'He's no chance,' she scoffed. 'Give me a strong and reliable copper any time. If I wanted an academic, there were plenty at Oxford gasping for a woman. Where would Howard be without you and me? Sad and lonely, that's where; never quite believing he's chosen the right world; only really happy when he sits down at that piano and releases his Mr Hyde.'

With money from the sale of his dead parents' house, Howard had bought a Steinway. As if offering a requiem to his father's inconsolable ghost, he played it every day, classics and jazz. While Clarice, who had Grade 8 piano, turned for him, he'd once rendered them both spellbound with Beethoven's *Appassionata*.

'O.K. Marina Scott,' he said. 'She was a true first and seemed a tough cookie. She'd argue white's black, black's white, just for the hell of it. Intelligent, well-read, and fearless, she'd pursue you after a lecture to discuss what you said; scared some colleagues shitless. They'd scurry out of the lecture hall and skulk in a senior common room for a couple of hours.'

'Jane Scott learned from somewhere Marina had a boyfriend. What about him?'

Howard didn't answer immediately; then said, 'Look, anything you get from me is not from me. *Compris?*'

'Sure.'

'Jonathan Puttman was the boyfriend; two-one in the old days, first nowadays, because we need to stay high in the league tables.'

'Like a football team.'

'Worse. Universities can fix the results. We're our own referees. Don't get me started. It's driving me crazy. Let's say Marina took Jonathan out of his comfort zone.'

'And after graduation?'

'He went on to do a Ph.D., which she should have done. Instead she washed her hands of the lot of us and worked on the checkouts at Sainsbury's.'

'That was it?'

'Well, he's now a schoolteacher in Islington. She disappeared in the spring after they both graduated.'

'Nobody wrote her a reference for anything?'

'Not that I know of, and I'm sure I'd have been her first referee. But there are a couple of other things.'

'Yeah?'

'Here's something known only to me. Just before Christmas, in that first term after her degree, when she was on the check-outs and Jonathan had begun his Ph.D., she suddenly came to my house one evening at about eight o'clock and more or less offered herself to me, while pretending she was considering a Ph.D. herself. It was before I met Cindy, you know.'

'What did you do?'

'I gave her some coffee, and we discussed her Ph.D. proposal, a feminist approach to D.H. Lawrence; both of us with a straight face in a crazy situation. Marina was sexy, you know; blond hair, like that Mrs Scott who came to see me; great body likewise. There she was saying, "Take me", while, off the top of my head, I'm bullshitting about feminism and Lady Chatterley. After over an hour I drove her back to the flat she shared with Jonathan. She really was desperate; tough cookie was all surface.'

How could it not be, he thought. She must have known what her mother did for a living, and she'd been disowned by her father.

'The other thing?'

'Something most people knew. No sooner had I got her back to the flat than she and Jonathan discovered they'd won a trip to Paris, first class Eurostar, five star hotel.'

'Blimey!'

'A competition, all over the media; Citroën or Renault, I can't remember which, various prizes.' He paused, and then continued, 'What does Bogart say to Ingrid Bergman in

Casablanca, "We'll always have Paris"? Maybe the Paris trip was it for Marina and Jonathan too. They went in the spring, 1998, then broke up. Jonathan went on to complete his Ph.D. on time, got a job, married, and now his wife is with child. He keeps in touch for reference purposes. All he ever said of Marina was that she'd decided to move to London, and he'd lost track of her. It can happen in any relationship. Who knows better than me?'

'You'll give me the school where Jonathan Puttman teaches?'

'Yeah, OK, all as long as I'm kept out of it. But why so much interest in Marina? You've told me she's not reported missing. I thought you were snowed under with Farmwell-Pembury. Where's Marina's parents?'

'Mother dead, father unknown; brought up independently of her mother with money from the mystery father. But now there's a pile of money waiting for her from the dead mother. Her granddad was a postman and a wonderful swimmer. He organised a swimming club at the local baths; taught Clarice and me, and most of the kids I knew to swim, all free of charge.'

'More of your Atherstone past.'

'Yeah.'

'You always think you owe it something?'

'I'm just helping a friend.'

Howard nodded in appreciation, before saying, 'Marina, you know. She's in Shakespeare's *Pericles*. She's lost, but then she's found. Even working in a brothel, she remains virtuously virgin. The play ends full of harmony.'

14

Caroline ('Call Cal') Edmondson knew the man on the next exercise bike was checking her out, glancing from the corner of his eyes at her boobs, and then turning his head for his full money's worth, when he thought she was gazing straight ahead and unaware of him. It was as if she had been considerately placed there by the gym management as his personal page 3 to relieve the strain of his work-out. Twisting her left hand on the handlebar grip to reveal her engagement ring, she wondered if she should tell Dominic about this kind of randy attention. Competition might rouse him to be his old self, even if it was no more than lust for any reasonably shaped young woman in leotard and tights. The night before he left for Iraq was better, but it was still only a feeble thrill for her, and nothing at all for him after the foreplay, though he said he didn't mind, 'As long as I'm starting to make you happy again.'

Side by side on their backs afterwards, their naked bodies lightly touching as they both gazed doubtfully at the ceiling of the bedroom of her flat in Sevenoaks, she asked, 'Are you worried about Iraq?'

'Why should I be? It's what we've all been trained for.'

He lay silently beside her, almost as if she weren't there, eventually declaring, as if speaking to himself, 'I'll be back to what I was, when it's all over.'

Back with his great, powerful body; her friend, Sally, slight as a blade of grass, exclaiming last summer, 'My God, look at the size of him; all that on top of you!'

He was on leave, and they were both watching him 'muscling in with the men,' as he liked to call it. Wearing only very short shorts and boots, and blatantly relishing the burning sun, he was spending the afternoon working for his father's company, 'Mitchams Marquees', erecting a marquee for Sally's brother's twenty-first. Six foot four and sixteen stones, he played lock for his rugby club, and when the work was finished, he started a passing game with the men, using a canvas bag for a ball; all of them, stripped to the waist, eventually falling into a laughing, tangled heap.

'Come on, Mark. Join in. You're big enough,' he yelled to her uncle Mark, who'd arrived to make sure all the booze for the party was sorted.

'Too physical for me,' Mark called back, turning and suggestively raising his eyebrows to Sally and herself.

She pushed harder on the peddles, sure the columns of lights on the little screen in front of her must now be indicating the mountainous stage of the programme, though she didn't look to confirm this. Better always to press on, let your mind drift, and hope, when you did glance at the screen, you were already through the toughest stretches. Look too soon, you might still be in the foothills and already feeling drained, depending on the day you'd had.

Not good for her today with Mick, the station boss, raging all over the studio, as if he intended to bring on one of her migraines.

'I take a fucking week off, and everybody fucks up!'

He meant her, 'Call Cal.'

'Call Cal' about anything happening within and around

the M25.

The station was easy-listening music with chat and phone-ins. A kitten, spun undamaged in a washing-machine, prompted calls about gerbils, rabbits, tortoises, all with the same dizzying CV.

Every day a clamour for attention, explanations, solutions, distractions: 'Stretch-marks,' 'Osama bin Laden', 'Man-boobs,' 'George W Bush,' 'Tattoos,' 'Camilla as Queen,' 'Paedophiles,' 'Brand-Beckham,' 'Immigration,' 'House-husbands.'

A chaos of subjects and views, interrupted by Tariq on sport, and by all the never changing turmoil to do with traffic and weather: lorries shedding loads, caravans overturning, multi-vehicle pile-ups in rain, fog, and ice.

Everybody lost unless they could connect instantly by phone with somebody.

The idea coming from nowhere, she asked people stuck in traffic jams to 'Call Cal with your story; not just about traffic, but about life.'

'Fantastic,' Mick said, 'cars as confession boxes. Personal stuff's what we're all about, especially people up against it. We all need the boost of knowing we're ahead of somebody. It's why we can't have enough of people stranded at airports, sleeping on floors, bogs overflowing, clean underwear already checked in with the luggage. They're taking a holiday, and we're shagging ourselves; serves the bastards right.'

But she took her idea further. While Mick was away, 'for a procedure so I can pee without sitting down,' she announced a 'Loss of the Month' competition. Whose traffic delay cost them most that month: a job, a flight, a relationship? Fincham sponsorship offered a prize of a lunch for two at a Fincham pub, drinks excluded.

Phone lines were jammed. Record audience-figures, while a man recounted being stuck for four hours where the M2 from Kent meets the approach to the Dartford Tunnel, and when he was trying to battle his way around the M25, then up the M1 and M6 to his parents' golden wedding celebrations in Carlisle, most of which he missed. He recalled the complete standstill: motorists sharing food, water, cigarettes, and jokes; a great-grandma remembering the Blitz; and right next to him a woman called Susannah in a Toyota Avensis, who'd never returned his texts, nor the Dusty Springfield CD he'd passed over to her, telling her (which was true, no kidding) he actually was the son of a Methodist preacher-man.

Laughs all around the studio, till suddenly a hysterical mum burst onto the airwaves and revealed her nineteen years old daughter had lost a leg and half an arm in the accident the man was entertaining everybody with.

Phones suddenly overwhelmed with tales of road carnage, deaths and mutilations nobody wanted to hear about. A listener called her 'Callous Cal,' and Mick came back into a fire-storm from all the sponsors, Fincham included.

'Another stunt like that, you're finished,' he bellowed at her this morning, standing behind his desk in his shoe box of an office, Tariq having told her it was painful for him to sit down, and he still couldn't hit the bowl standing up. 'No amount of Farmwell-Pembury and Fincham and uncle Mark will let you through the door of this fucking station. We're about feel-good, relief-massage for people who never get anything up. It's not about immersing them in their fucking misery.'

'You're saying I'm only here because of my family, and now

all the sensation about uncle Mark's murder!'

'Christ, have you seen the girls out there with a B.A., a chat-up voice, and a mountain of student debt. You can net them like fish in a barrel; so called ready for anything new women, service industry slaves, blow-dry/blow-job.'

No answer to that, so she waited for him to calm down. Five women under thirty in the station, he hasn't made a pass at any of us. Dominic could pick him up under one arm and crush him.

After a minute or so, she challenged, 'Do I still have a job here?'

'Just.'

The word for mummy's and daddy's marriage she thought, stepping down from the exercise bike to begin her warm-down and admire her reflection in the gym's wall of mirrors. It's 'just' surviving, probably only till the death of granddad Edmondson in New Zealand. Mummy must have taken the Australian trip, because she can't keep up the pretence in front of all the New Zealand relatives. She's been like a zombie since uncle Mark's murder. Must feel guilty, telling him he sickened her. All work for her, all pleasure for him, and for daddy with Cambridge Katherine. Why doesn't mummy see a gynaecologist, if sex is so painful for her?

Love should be forever, like grandma Penelope's love for Peter Burgess.

The old photograph album she looked through with grandma Penelope: Peter Burgess smiling in his cricket whites, Peter Burgess and grandma Penelope holding hands at their first dance party, and looking as much in love with each other as two people could ever be; more in love than ever mummy and daddy looked, or grandma Penelope and granddad Christopher. Grandma Penelope still had the dress she wore for that dance, and it still fitted her, 'skimming the figure,' as she liked to say.

She drove grandma Penelope to that pub near Lewis, where they asked to see the big bedroom overlooking the garden at the back.

'All new furniture and new wallpaper,' grandma Penelope said, 'but everything in the same place.'

Sitting on the bed, grandma Penelope covered her face with her hands and cried like a little girl.

Relax, she told herself, lying on a mat, the man from the next exercise bike almost striding over her, his smile down at her seeking intimacy.

What might he be like as a husband? How many men should a woman try out? Suppose Dominic was killed in Iraq?

That policeman hunting for uncle Mark's murderer; his wife was killed in that dreadful hit-and-run. Interviewed on TV, unmarked, he looked as if he no longer inhabited the earth.

'She was living. She was dead,' he said. 'There was no in-between.'

15

Warne phoned Jonathan Puttman's school at lunchtime, the day after seeing Howard. He asked the school secretary to tell Dr Puttman not to be alarmed. 'It's just that he might be able to help me with some information. And please keep this call confidential.'

'Hello, Dr Puttnam here.'

'Oh, hello. My name's David Warne. I'm a chief inspector with Canterbury CID. Nothing for you to worry about, but I'm trying to locate a former student at Canterbury University. It's a Marina Scott, and I'm wondering if you could help me. I understand she was your girl-friend, when you were both students.'

'Marina Scott! Is this a joke? We broke up after we graduated, nearly six years ago. I haven't seen or heard from her since. I'm married now, and my wife's expecting a baby. This call scared me to death. I thought something was going wrong with her pregnancy.'

'Look, I'm sorry to drop on you like this. Could we meet somewhere? If I could talk to you about Marina, it might give me some clue as to what might have happened to her.'

'Is she in trouble?'

'Not that I know of. In fact she's likely to come into money and property, if we can find her.'

'I'm not sure Marina needs money.'

'What do you mean?'

'Sorry. Nothing. I shouldn't have said that. Look, are you the detective who's in charge of that homosexual murder case in Chilham?'

'That's me. I'm impressed you know about it.'

'It's national news, and I've seen you on TV. I remember your name because of Shane Warne, you know, the Aussie bowler. I still follow things in Canterbury. I lived there till I got this job in Islington.'

'Well, how about meeting me? Just to take me up to when you and Marina parted. I can come up to London. Let me buy you a lunch.'

'Looks like I'm being made an offer I can't refuse. Sometimes I'm glad I've forgotten all about Marina. Then I wonder what happened to her. My wife knows about her and me as students, so there's no problem there.'

'Good.'

The following Sunday he was on a train to London to meet Jonathan Puttnam for lunch at the National Gallery, a table for two booked in Warne's name.

He read in *The Observer* about United's game the previous day; 3-1 against Blackburn, Van Nistelrooy 1, Scholes 2; United still top of the Premiership; everything better than last season, when Fergie screwed up, saying he was retiring. He felt guilty in the comfort of the train. For an afternoon in London on an April day like this he'd have pressed Clarice to use the bike, 'Less than an hour, we're in the middle of the city.'

Howard taking the piss.

'Machismo schmizmo. You carry Clarice away on that great beast like Sir Galahad on his charger.'

'Get yourself a bike, Howard, get yourself a girl,' Clarice

teased, posing alongside the bike, one hand on her hip, the other behind her head. 'But it's a pain arriving everywhere in leathers.'

'You look great in leathers,' Howard said.

On the train he fantasised her back into life, the red leathers clinging to her like a second skin, her face direct and challenging beneath her dark, short-cropped, brown hair. Astride their mighty BMW 1200 GT, he watched her walk to straddle behind him, waiting for the sexy opening of her legs as she mounted, her eight and a half stones barely registering on the bike's suspension.

In bed the tips of his fingers gently pushed through her hair to caress her scalp.

'Hair like mine, you might be thinking you're with a bloke.'

'Not with these breasts, and what I'm touching now between your legs.'

So vivid, he was getting a hard-on, even while he heard her protests about their last trip to Belgium and France.

'Why don't we go by Eurostar? We're in our forties for God's sake.'

Her words an open wound in his heart.

'We can tour around on the bike. We've got good hotels. I've booked great restaurants. We can spend all evening eating and drinking.'

A trip partly to do with the First World War; so plenty of death.

Ypres and then Lille.

Standing with hundreds of others at the Menin Gate at eight o'clock on a Saturday evening, while the Last Post was played; a prelude to one of the great dinners, and following a day exploring Ypres and its market, and visiting nearby First World War cemeteries.

Tyne Cot, the largest Commonwealth cemetery in the world; Langemark, their first ever encounter with a German cemetery.

'Just a graveyard,' he said, responding to Langemark's sombre functionality, the complete absence of commemoration; black rectangular gravestones flat on the ground, recording several bodies in each grave. 'In France, and at Tyne Cot today, it's like being in a peaceful garden; overwhelming, but you can think there are plenty of worse places to end up.'

'Just a brooding, even menacing, sense of the end here,' she said. 'No claim that anything makes sense.'

'Burial pits, get rid of the bodies. Belgium wouldn't allow German headstones to be upright. Revenge, I suppose. Not many Germans come here.'

She thought a moment and then said, 'You're saying we acclaim all our dead, because we won?'

'Acclaim? What do you mean, acclaim all that death?

'*They shall grow not old.*'

While he moved to the next flat gravestone to contemplate several more German names, she continued the famous lines, '*They shall grow not old, as we that are left grow old: / Age shall not weary them, nor the years condemn.*'

'According to the poet,' she continued, taking hold of his hand, 'our fallen soldiers are better off heroically dead, because they will miss all the trials of later life.'

'Sentimental,' he responded bitterly. 'Always said at the cenotaph by some well fed tosser, enjoying his three score and ten.'

'It's the religiosity I can't stand; all that fatalistic worship of human sacrifice, as if it's the best we Brits are capable of; as if we can't wait for the next occasion.'

'It's here already with Bush and Blair and Iraq. Didn't Bush's family make sure he avoided Vietnam? And what does Blair know about fighting in a war? They should both come here; see the result.'

'It's just as likely to inspire them to bear a leader's burdens, right a wrong; kill to prevent more killing. So it goes on all sides. There's never a war to end all wars. In June 1940, Hitler is one German who did come here.'

Looking down at the gravestone, he remembered his dad, rescued from Dunkirk; 'pulled out o` sea wi` mi` `air like a drownin` rat.'

'I joined the police,' he said, 'to keep the show on the road, help everybody to live together, but I'd never want to fight in any war.'

'Caught up in something monstrous like the young men buried here; all the possibilities of your life wasted.'

But when they were back at the bike and she was putting on her helmet, he sensed an anguished change of mood in her, hearing her say, as if speaking to herself, '*Kill, kill, kill, kill, kill, kill!*'

'What's that?'

'Lear, near the end of the play, tormented by what he may need to do, what any of us may need to do. The First World War may not have been inevitable, but Hitler certainly had to be defeated. Pacifism would have been no good.'

Lille next day, exploring among other sights its spectacular *Grand-Place*, dedicated to General de Gaulle. Close to them at the next table during their late lunch were two young men, obviously gay. Standing up to leave, they kissed each other on the lips before they parted, one of them saying defiantly, '*Liberté, Egalité Fraternité, ou La Mort.*'

'You get *la mort* in the end, no matter what' he said to Clarice, as they drank their coffee. 'There's no *ou* about it.'

Pathetic smart-arse, he thought now, on the train, tears in his eyes.

No wonder she was hardly listening to him; looking instead through the guide they'd bought to Lille's *Palais des Beaux-Arts*, and fixed on a beautiful Raphael drawing of a young woman, which had captured her earlier in their visit to the *Palais* itself. Was it prompting her to think of the drawing of herself by her mother's closest friend, Clarice Pomeroy? Done when she was eighteen and Oxford bound, he'd recognised, even at the time, how full it was of the older women's passionate involvement in her young promise, the kind of promise stifled in themselves. Seeing it in her study, Howard read Clarice Pomeroy's signature and exclaimed, 'So that explains your name! I always thought it might have something to do with Clarice Cliff. You know, the ceramic artist. I saw some Clarice Pomeroy paintings in Manchester Art Gallery, when I was up there as an external examiner. The girl at the piano in one of them looks just like you.'

On the train he heard Clarice's reply, word for word.

'The other three paintings in Manchester are of my mother: ironing, sewing, washing her hair. My mother and Clarice Pomeroy were close friends from their childhood. They use to take motorbike trips together on Clarice's BSA 250. Clarice always wanted to celebrate women, even in domestic situations. She thought there was too much resignation in Lowry.'

Who could have known *la mort* was so near to that lunch in

Lille's *Grand-Place*? Who could have foreseen Clarice, ten hours later, smashed onto the grass verge alongside Canterbury's Rheims Way, flowering plants in pots scattered around her in the darkness?

Plants bought on the market at Ypres.

So they wouldn't be crushed in the bike's panniers, she'd been holding some of them in plastic bags against his back.

He'd give anything to have her growing old beside him.

16

'I don't usually eat Sunday lunch in this kind of style,' Jonathan Puttnam said.

He was slim, just below Warne's height; good casual clothes, a full head of brown hair; wedding ring; at the outset of family life.

'Me neither,' Warne replied. 'A sandwich does me usually. But this will last me all day, and I might have a snooze on the train going back.'

They both ordered sea bass.

'My dad always advised me to go for the fish in restaurants,' Warne said, as he tasted the over-priced Chardonnay. '"Order steak", he'd say; "you'll have to chew it till your teeth fall out".'

'Did he know about food?'

'Not much, he was a flagger. He laid flag-stones, what we call paving-slabs nowadays. He was very fast. Building sites competed for him; all hammer and chisel work; like Michael Angelo my wife used to joke. Then angle-grinders were invented.'

He could see he'd lost Jonathan Puttnam, who drank some of the wine before saying, 'The death of your wife in Canterbury was something else I followed on the news. With your involvement in the homosexual murder it made me take you seriously, when you phoned.'

'Right.'

'It was a phone call I tried to convince myself would never

happen, but I wasn't surprised when it did. I suppose the past never goes away.'

'Depends,' Warne said, sipping more wine. 'But if we're going to get straight on to Marina, tell me what happened on that Paris trip? Thinking about the two of you, that Paris jaunt looks like some sort of key.'

'So, you know about Paris. I used to wish we'd never won that prize, but if it hadn't been Paris, I'm sure it would have been something else.'

'What happened?'

'Marina happened, all her contempt for the way life is. In one of our seminars, you know, she took apart a horny young lecturer's reading of Marvell's *To His Coy Mistress*, telling him to his face he'd no idea about the relationship between carnality and death, and that a man fucking a virgin woman was the genesis of all violations.'

'That must have been some seminar.'

'Yeah, but it wasn't always like that. She could be so funny. She published a spoof of Andrew Motion's poem, *To Whom It May Concern*, in the student English magazine. Motion's poem, you know, begins, *This poem about ice cream*. Her first line was, *This poem about a wet-dream*. She argued all Motion's poems were wet-dreams. He's the poet laureate, you know.'

'I know who the poet laureate is. I did a degree in English myself.'

'Oh, so you're a kind of Morse.'

'Does Morse have an English degree? Anyway, he's not real. Let's get back to Marina.'

Jonathan Puttnam drank some more wine, before saying, 'After we graduated, she started to steal.'

'How? Where from?'

'From Sainsbury's at first, where she worked. Food for us to eat, even though we had enough money to buy it; clothes from department stores. I was on edge. I didn't know how to stop her. I was too frightened to tell anyone. I thought I might be implicated. She stole T-shirts for me.'

'Was she on drugs, financing a habit?'

'No chance. She despised drug addicts, single mothers, fat people, anybody who lost control. She wouldn't touch alcohol.'

Warne shared out more wine as the food arrived.

'So what was Marina's motive for stealing,' he asked.

'To be ahead of the game, contempt again, power. She was always hoping there'd be a life-changing moment to raise her above everyone. Not knowing about her father made her feel life had played her a dirty trick, so why shouldn't she have her revenge? She never spoke about her mother.'

'And Paris brought all this to a head?'

'She was on a high all weekend; wanting to sneak away from *brasseries* without paying; stealing sexy underwear from *Galerie Lafayette*; posing in it in the bedroom, like a stripper; taunting me because she knew I was too miserable to have sex with her. Then on the way back she walked off the train at Ashford with a young man's bag. When she forced it open in the flat, it contained more than a million pounds in used notes.'

'Bloody hell!'

'It was a nightmare. The man's bag was overhead, next to ours. We were all in first class, and he was asleep, pissed with too much wine on top of drugs. When we reached Ashford, I took our bag and went off first. I only noticed she had another bag, when were on the platform. I couldn't get her to hand it back as a mistake, and then the train left. Back in the flat she thought this was the moment she'd always dreamed of. She started making plans about going to South America, where she could use her Spanish. I just sat there horrified. I put the telly on to drive it all out of my mind. Every news channel was talking about a young man getting off Eurostar at Waterloo, running up and down the platform crying out about a lost bag, and then throwing himself under an incoming train.'

Jesus Christ, Warne thought, Paul Sewell's suicide! It's down to Marina fucking Scott! It sent Maurice Sewell over the edge. He killed and killed - killed Clarice!

'Eat some food,' he almost commanded.

He remembered it had been over a week before the identity of the man jumping under the train was disclosed, but there'd never, ever, been any mention of money in the bag; just comments about the would-be actor's severe depression after failing several auditions.

A one-off for Sewell, letting his son be a bag-man; see if he could do it?

Paul knowing he'd fucked up big time; let his dad down; lost over a million quid; end it all.

'I became desperate,' Jonathan interrupted Warne's thoughts. 'I told Marina the man's death was our responsibility, but she argued it put us in the clear. The man must be guilty of something, so why shouldn't we have the money? With him dead, it could never be traced back to us, and, anyway, he was unidentified, and there was no mention of money in the missing bag. I told her she was mad. People didn't just forget over a million pounds, but if she wanted the money she could have it, and I'd move out and say nothing. I spent all night packing.

He drank more wine before saying, 'After I left next morning I never saw her again.'

'You know who the young man was who committed suicide,' Warne said.

'Later, it was all over the news about his father's alleged underworld connections.'

'Forget alleged. You know nothing more about Marina and the money?'

Jonathan Puttnam waited until the waiter collected their plates before answering.

'Five days after the suicide a man appeared at my new digs. He knew all about how Marina had stolen the bag and what was in it. He said he had CCTV tape of us quarrelling at Ashford station. He even knew the numbers of our seats on Eurostar.'

'Was he a copper?'

'He wouldn't identify himself. He came to see me, because Marina wasn't in the flat. I had to admit what had happened. He said if Marina returned the money, we could put the whole thing to bed, forget about it. That was just what I wanted to hear.'

'Can you describe the man?'

'Chain-smoker; tall and thin, completely bald, pencil moustache, three-piece suit; very polite and friendly; but get on his wrong side, he'd know how to break you. After he'd sat on my bed, I didn't want to sleep in it that night.'

Joe Pawsey, on another mission for Maurice Sewell.

'Davy boy,' Pawsey said to him in the eighties, 'a provincial northern lad like you should build his career outside London.'

'Am I in trouble?' Jonathan Puttnam asked, before putting a spoon into his *crème caramel*.

'Maybe,' Warne said, eating his lemon tart without tasting it. 'You've certainly concealed a crime.'

'Oh God, I'm a schoolteacher, my wife too. We've a baby on the way.'

'Let's not get ahead of ourselves. What happened to Marina's still a mystery, and it's Marina I'm interested in. Maybe she returned the money, and we can forget about it. You could be in the clear.'

'She wouldn't have returned it for nothing. She'd have wanted something for it. I know her.'

'And I know something about the people she'd got involved with. They wouldn't be impressed by piss-takes of the poet laureate, and there's nothing they don't know about carnality and death.'

They finished their desserts in silence. As they drank their coffee, Warne said, 'I'll do my very best for you.'

'Thanks. What shall I tell my wife?'

'Anything that doesn't make her worry.'

Parting at the main entrance to the National Gallery, they shook hands, Jonathan Puttnam slowly stepping down into Trafalgar Square, but Warne returning to the gallery itself, thoughts spinning.

F-Ps, father and son, involved with the Sewells, father and son; and now, out of nowhere, Marina Scott's in the mix, and maybe Mark's killer too, if he could find the connection. Fuck it! Admit it, you stupid bastard! You need Pawsey, even if his shit comes with him. He'll know about Maurice Sewell and the F-Ps, and he must have hunted Marina down, so he'll know what happened to her.

Oh to escape all this and be with Clarice again! Their early life together, so innocent!

He searched out Vermeer's *A Young Woman Standing at a Virginal.*

They were both sixteen, and Clarice had passed her grade 8 piano exam with distinction. In celebration Clarice Pomeroy had done a painting, 'after Vermeer,' of Clarice standing at the upright piano in her 'studio', actually the front room of the terrace house she shared with her father, whose leg was blown off in the First World War. It was one of the paintings Howard had seen in Manchester.

'As near to Vermeer, as I can get,' Clarice Pomeroy said, 'and that's miles away.'

True, he thought, as he now looked again at the Vermeer in the National Gallery. Clarice Pomeroy's painting was altogether simpler. Unlike Vermeer's it had no window, no chair, no other paintings in it; and unlike Vermeer's richly dressed girl, Clarice was wearing a white, short-sleeved, blouse and blue skirt, though you could see a stitched pattern on the blouse, and light was catching Clarice's necklace of blue, glass beads.

And you, my love, he said to himself, look as though you know something about the keys you're touching, but Vermeer's girl doesn't. She looks as if she's been dressed up for the pose and wants to make sure she holds it for the painter.

Who was the girl in Vermeer's painting? Was it ever Vermeer's intention to preserve her actual life? Clarice Pomeroy wanted to preserve Clarice's actual life and to celebrate that Grade 8 pass, though in her painting too there was faking. Clarice, in fact, would never play the piano in the studio, because 'the keys stick, and it's hopelessly out of tune.' Like Vermeer's girl, she too was posing.

As she does forever in my memory, he thought, turning to leave the National Gallery; alive but not alive; imprisoned in scenes we can never move on from.

17

'Gillian Edmondson's never even been in New Zealand!'
Warne's immediate announcement to Liz, as she came into his office the Tuesday after his trip to London. Pressed by her, he'd phoned the police in Christchurch, South Island, late the previous evening.

'Wow! So what does that mean? You're really sure she's not there?'

'I spoke to a superintendent in Christchurch. The Edmondsons are a very prominent family in the Waipara Hills wine region about thirty miles north of Christchurch. When Ralph Edmondson arrived from the UK, it was big local news; photographs in the paper, TV; but there's never been any sign or mention of Gillian.'

'Can this be connected to Mark's murder?'

'Dunno. It may just be a marriage break-up. We know Ralph Edmondson was with his woman in Cambridge the night of Mark's murder, even though it's a bloke who's vouching for him.'

'But why would Gillian disappear? She could have just called an end to the marriage and let Ralph fly away.'

'Assuming she's not dead herself, maybe she wanted to drop everything round the necks of Ralph and the rest of the family. She's spent the best part of her life holding Farmwell-Pembury enterprises together, while everybody else in the family's been having a good time. Suppose she decided to drop out.'

'I'd rather think that than think she's been killed, or become a killer herself.'

'Can you see her involved in Mark's murder. Where's the motive?'

'Do you think we'd better talk to the daughter, "Call Cal"?'

'Yeah. I gave the superintendent in Christchurch an idea of what we're involved in. I told him to tell Ralph Edmondson to contact his daughter and tell her about her mother. I said we'd be doing that tomorrow, even if Ralph didn't. I've also decided to search the Edmondsons' house in Chilham.'

'Search-warrant?'

'Yeah.   '

'Who's going to tell the F-Ps about all this?'

'Caroline can tell them about her mother. I don't care who tells them about the search-warrant.'

'Wherever Gillian is, she'll need money.'

'So we go all the way, into her bank accounts. If she's withdrawing from cash-points, we have her whereabouts.'

'I'll chase the money.'

'Great. Listen, Liz. I'm going for broke on this. I want to open the F-Ps up, see what's inside their shell. If there's nothing bad, or not much that's bad, I could be finished. They'll go for me, especially if we haven't found Mark's killer. But I want you to understand, I'll make sure everyone knows it's all my responsibility. I'll make sure you're not damaged.'

Liz waited a few seconds, before she said, 'Thanks for that. But I've never not trusted you.'

Left alone, he phoned Cunningham in Maidstone.

'Gillian Edmondson's not with her husband in New Zealand. She's missing. Nobody knows where she is. I'm getting a search-warrant to search the Edmondsons' house in Chilham.'

'Are you out of your mind?'

'I don't think so. Why is she missing?'

'You're not suggesting she killed her brother?'

'I'm not suggesting anything. She could be dead herself. Our job is to find things out.'

'You've not found much lately.'

'You bastard.'

'I'll put that on report.'

'Suit yourself.'

For lunch he ate a home-made sandwich at his desk. Recalling his lunch in The White Hart, with Jane Scott sitting opposite him, he knew he wanted to share more of her life. He remembered his phone call to her the evening they parted on the station platform.

'I just wanted to say I'm glad you said what you said.'

'That makes me glad,' she responded. 'I was thinking I might have embarrassed you, as well as loading work on you you didn't need.'

'You'll never embarrass me, and I've already found out who Marina's boy-friend was. I'm going to arrange to see him. I'll get back to you, as soon as I've any real news. Don't ever think I've forgotten you.'

'Oh, I'm so happy to hear that.'

Would Jonathan Puttnam's revelations last Sunday, and whatever he eventually learned from Joe Pawsey keep her happy? Pawsey must have tracked Marina down. He knew Marilyn, because she serviced Sewell, so he must have been amazed to recognise Marina as Marilyn's daughter. The photograph Jane had left showed she looked just like her mother. No resemblance to Sewell though, so who was the father?

Waiting for the right time to phone New Zealand yesterday evening, he'd phoned Pawsey at his house in Chalfont St Giles. Barbara, his wife, happened to be at her book-reading group, so there were lots of 'fucks' from Pawsey, who boasted of never swearing in the presence of his wife and three daughters, and of never even looking at other women.

'Fuck it, Davy boy, why do you want more of Maurice Sewell? He's as good as banged up for life. Don't give him any more fucking aggravation. He's time on his hands all day in his cell, time and money. He can buy somebody to do anything.'

He's already had your wife killed was implicit.

'Uxorious,' Clarice used to say of Pawsey, and he was fascinated by her.

'No more of the "Davy boy" crap. You mean he had my wife killed.'

Silence.

'I want to know what happened to Marina Scott, when you found her with Paul Sewell's money.'

'What the fuck are you talking about!'

'Don't horse-shit me. I've spoken to Jonathan Puttnam, who was on that Paris trip with her. He's told me about you sitting on his bed and smoking and screwing his confession out of him.'

'Fuck off. I'll deny it all.'

'Then I'll come after you with a statement from Jonathan Puttnam. Accuse you of complicity in my wife's murder, because of your protection of Maurice Sewell. If it costs me my job, I don't give a shit. I've lost Clarice. What else is there for me to lose? I'll just make sure *you* lose and Barbara loses, and your fucking house is smeared with Sewell's bribes, because you'll be exposed, whether any of it sticks or not. I should have done it years ago. So tell me about Marina Scott, or else! I know she was Marilyn Scott's daughter.'

'Christ!'

'Tell me!'

'Not on the fucking phone. Come up and see me next Sunday afternoon. Barbara's playing badminton.'

You menaced Pawsey by wading into his sewer.

Finishing a banana, he re-played his confrontation with Pawsey in Pawsey's office, when his transfer out of the Met finally came through; Pawsey sitting behind his desk, listening to him yelling.

'You think it's a fucking game.'

Pawsey staying calm; a wanker on his team. Get rid of him.

'A fucking game, Davy boy, is exactly what it is. Nothing matters except you and me get a result.'

Letting this sink in, he went on, 'Crime's just life taking a shit. It's always going to happen. I assumed you knew that, Davy boy, with all that education behind you.'

'Maurice Sewell gives us losers, so we don't go after him.'

'He gives us results, Davy boy.'

Results. Results. Results. Warne lobbed the banana skin into a rubbish bin in the corner of his office. Football managers say 'a result,' as long as they don't lose. And Howard was revealing his job depended on 'results,' favourable presentations of university success, whatever the reality. Bush and Blair too needed a 'result' in Iraq. Eventually, they would contrive one and proclaim it, leaving facts to sort themselves out.

Late in the afternoon, a knock on his door, and Liz came in

accompanying a very distraught looking Caroline Edmondson.

'"Call Cal",' Liz said, after introducing Caroline by her full name. 'A lively programme. Are you "Cal" outside the studio?'

'It's what everybody calls me.'

'OK if we use it?'

'Sure.'

'You're getting married in the cathedral,' Warne intervened.

'Yes, but my fiancé's in Iraq. He was in the battle for Basra. He's a captain with the Seventh Armoured Brigade.'

'"Mitcham's Marquees",' Warne said.

'The company Dominic's father founded. But Dominic wanted to achieve something for himself; not simply slip into his dad's shoes, as he used to say.'

'Well, his dad's likely to wear his shoes for quite a long time yet. He can't be much older than me.'

'Look, you must know I'm not here to talk about "Mitcham's Marquees",' Caroline suddenly insisted, tears appearing. 'I had a phone call from my father first thing this morning. He told me my mother's not with him in New Zealand, and that you know this. He's preparing a statement with his lawyer. He's going to fax it to you. I've no idea what's going on.'

'We just want to find out where you're mother is.'

'Why? You surely can't think she's anything to do with uncle Mark's murder!'

'What did your father tell you on the phone?' Liz asked.

'That my mother deserted him at Heathrow. She never boarded the plane to New Zealand. As they were going to check in the luggage, she took her suitcase and announced she was leaving him, moving to live somewhere on her own.'

'So he flew out alone?' Liz continued.

'Yes. He's told his family in New Zealand the marriage is under strain, but will get back to normal when he's back in England, and they've had a break from each other.'

'Did your mother say where she was going?' Warne asked.

'No. '

'So nobody's any idea where she is?'

'No.'

'How did your mother get on with Mark?' Liz asked.

Caroline thought about this, until she said, 'Not well, though it wasn't all uncle Mark's fault. He would have signed any truce. She simply couldn't bear his promiscuity, and her hostility to him became worse when daddy began his affairs, which I'm sure you know about. He was with "Cambridge Katherine" (mummy's term) the night uncle Mark was killed. She's a philosophy professor.'

'Yes, we know about her,' Warne said.

Again Caroline insisted, 'You can't believe mummy's involved in uncle Mark's murder. She didn't despise him that much. She thought too much about the family. She wanted to keep it together, as much for my sake as anybody else's. Dominic's family, you know, are very Christian, very big in the cathedral.'

'We'd like you to tell your grandparents about your parents,' Warne said.

'My father's already asked me to do that.'

'Poor "Call Cal",' Liz said later. 'She's full of happiness on the radio.'

'We'd better check all the family phone and email records to be sure Cal's telling the truth, and her mother hasn't made contact.'

'Sir Christopher's going to love this.'

'He's only ever loved himself.'

18

'No WMD, so far,' Howard said, thoughtfully sipping his *Mersault-Charmes, Premier Cru,* before carefully pushing his fork into his last piece of roast chicken.

'Before Robin Cook resigned from Blair's cabinet,' Warne responded, 'he claimed we were only daring to attack Iraq because we knew Saddam didn't have WMD.'

'The three of us sound like a TV satirical sketch,' Cindy said.

She sat opposite Warne, Howard at the head of the table. They were eating in his house on Sunday evening, Warne having arrived directly from seeing Pawsey.

'What?' Howard said.

'Well, listen to us,' Cindy insisted, 'discussing terrible events thousands of miles away, while enjoying all these comforts.'

'Blair told parliament Saddam's WMD could be ready for use in forty-five minutes,' Howard responded. 'That's not so far away.'

'Neither of us believed Blair,' Cindy retorted.

'Islam would sure put an end to this *Mersault*,' Warne declared, admiring again the wine's wonderful golden-yellow colour, and then, as it slipped demandingly over his palate, attempting to distinguish all the flavours (almond, pineapple, peach, apple, nut) Howard had alerted him to. Relishing the *Mersault* anaesthetised what he learned about Marina Scott from Pawsey this afternoon. It made it easier to keep up a front before Howard. 'A true first,' Howard had said of Marina. Now, according to Pawsey, she was sure to be a true corpse.

'I don't think Bush was thinking of defending *Mersault,* when he warned about the axis of evil,' Howard said, emptying the bottle into Warne's glass.

'Is even the axis of evil true?' Cindy came back.

'"Well, if good men do nothing, evil prospers",' Howard said, signalling comic quotation marks.

'Who's defining good and evil?' Cindy challenged.

'Look,' Howard persisted, 'I know we're children of Europe's longest ever period of peace, but enemies always exist. That's basic history. And the US will have them, whether it wants them or not. Living and breathing and moving about it shakes other nations up; more than ever nowadays, with Cold War won and the USSR finished.'

'But invading Iraq wasn't accidental,' Cindy responded. 'It was deliberate, like Vietnam, another terrible blunder; all that killing to prevent the spread of communism, and what are we now left with in that country, a one party communist state!'

'What can I say?' Howard pleaded in self-mockery. 'All great nations do great wrong.'

'But we shouldn't be resigned to it.'

'It happens, whether we're resigned or not.'

Knowing Cindy had marched with two girl-friends on the London demo against the invasion of Iraq, Warne said, 'Wasn't the response to 9/11 supposed to be about Osama bin Laden? Why switch to Saddam? Except Clarice and I read Bush was planning to take Saddam out well before 9/11.'

'Howard knows it's the American Neo-Cons,' Cindy said. 'With the Cold War won they want to destroy one of Israel's enemies and re-shape the Middle-East to serve America's needs.

As they see it, 9/11 was just a violent insanity, no connection with whatever America might have done in the world.'

'Essentially, 9/11 has made no difference,' Howard said, finishing his glass before placing his hand on Cindy's.

'Made no difference?' Cindy protested.

'The America its attackers wanted to destroy has become even more confirmed in its sense of itself,' Howard said. Then, with more energy, 'Look, if 9/11 was a desperate striking-back, even out of self-respect, against American hegemony, it's failed, and shouldn't we be glad it's failed? America is our major ally, defending the fundamentals of what we in the West believe in.'

'Let's get back to Saddam,' Warne said, as Cindy looked doubtfully at Howard. 'Even accepting he's a menace, couldn't we have kept him in his box, kept him contained?'

Pawsey was back in his head, as he watched Howard again squeeze Cindy's hand, before standing up to clear the table.

'Me,' Pawsey said this afternoon, 'I'd have kept Saddam as our son-of-a-bitch. He attacked Kuwait, because he thought he *was* our son-of-bitch and could get away with it. We taught him he was wrong, and there was only so far he could go, so we had him where we wanted him. No need to go after the bastard to eliminate him. I used to tell you, everything's about having people where you want them and being where you want to be yourself. When I came home from work, I wanted to be in this house with Barbara and the girls.'

'Nobody denies Saddam's a savage oppressor of his people and a supporter of terrorism,' Howard said, gathering the plates together. 'Who knows if he could have been contained? But Blair's right. Europe needs America; America needs Europe, even if he went too far, intoxicated by American adulation.'

Assembling, one by one, the knives and forks on top of the plates, it was as if he needed to make himself finally clear. 'America saved Western Europe in two world wars and stayed committed, when Stalin had six million troops on its eastern borders; so I'm pro-American, even though I'm a liberal lefty. I know all about the horrors of its foundation: massacres of Native Americans, slavery, continuing racism. But we English introduced slavery into Virginia, and European settlers took the land from the Native Americans, so let's get off our high horse.' Lifting the plates from the table, he continued, 'Nobody knows more than Americans themselves about the horrors. That's why their arts are so self-exposing. Watching their movies, you can sometimes think America hates what it's become. They're so full of wilful self-destruction.'

On his way towards the kitchen, he called back over his shoulder, 'Never forget the great democracy of American music, jazz especially. Repressive regimes always hate it, because it's so liberating.'

Warne and Cindy remained at the table. They knew Howard would be content to be left alone to mix the salad and prepare the cheese.

Smiling uncertainly, Cindy drank a glass of water, saying, 'Get myself ready for the next bottle.'

With the cheese Howard had promised a 'mind-blowing, "96 *Margaux*."'

Warne was thinking how he should tell Jane what he'd learned from Pawsey about Marina. Prepare her on the phone, then go and see her? When? First thing tomorrow was the search of the Edmondsons' house.

'How's things for you?' Cindy asked, responding to his

troubled face.

'OK,' he forced a smile, 'but it's been a tough week.'

After a moment's silence, Cindy, as if prompted by Howard's last remark, said, 'I'll always miss the four of us singing.'

'Me too, though you all had to put up with my bass.'

'You were always in tune, good sound.'

Soothing to hear her appreciation; the kind of female intimacy he was missing. When he walked home later, she and Howard would go to bed together.

She was head of maths in a school in Faversham and a top soprano in Canterbury Chorale, where Clarice had been a star alto; a petite red-head, in her late thirties, always, Warne thought, looking great, usually in high-heels and shortish skirts. When Howard first got to know her, she'd left her partner of three years because, 'All he wanted from me was sex.'

'I loved all our Beatles songs,' she was saying, 'Simon and Garfunkel, Everly Brothers, ABBA, all those American musicals.'

'Yeah, Howard thumping out the guitar parts on the Steinway.'

'*Here's to you, Mrs Robinson,*' she half-sang with a giggle.

He laughed back, knowing she was poking fun at herself, because her name was Cindy Robinson.

'Is Cindy OK with the Mrs Robinson song?' he asked Howard after the early singing sessions with her.

'Takes it lying down,' Howard replied, 'and, speaking of which, you should hear her top C, when we really make it.' Then, weeks later, 'She wants to love and be loved, and I'm more than ready for that, David buddy. She doesn't mind our age difference, and I don't want to live without her. It's the best relationship I've ever had with a woman.'

I still want to love and be loved too, Warne was thinking, as Cindy said, 'So much trouble in the world, I need to hold on to happiness.' When he didn't respond, she added, 'Howard says Clarice was a great teacher.'

'Yeah, he read some of the essays of her sixth-formers; said they were already degree standard.'

'I wasn't kidding,' Howard said, coming in from the kitchen with the salad bowl, and announcing, 'water with this to get ready for the *Margaux*, a wine of the gods.'

Passing the salad bowl around, he suddenly announced gloomily, 'I've just had a row with the big boss, the University Vice Chancellor.'

'And?' Warne said.

'Corporate image and mega bucks are all he's interested in. We academics are just worker ants. As long as we score and earn big, who actually cares what we do, even if it's absolute bollocks, and, believe me, some of it is.'

Cindy and Warne looking up from their salad, he went on, 'The Vice Chancellor's about to retire, so I tried to get him back to fundamentals. I asked him if he agreed academics were the *raison d'être* of the university.'

Warne sneaked a smile at Cindy.

'H's a crafty sod, you know' Howard continued. 'He went all democratic on me. "What about the cleaners?" he said. "They're important too." This is a guy who's put half the cleaners and some other workers on zero hours contracts and negotiated himself a salary at least twice as big as the prime-minister's! According to him Blair's given universities an *El Dorado*, with endless money to be made out of the rise and rise of student fees.'

'Oh Howard, love,' Cindy responded, taking her turn to put a comforting hand on his, 'Everybody's being chased in their job; me at school, and David, I'm sure.'

'You bet,' Warne said, envious of Cindy's hand.

'Yeah,' Howard sighed, smiling longingly at Cindy, 'you're right.' Standing up, he sighed again, '*Margaux* and cheese time. I've chosen mild cheeses. You don't want strong cheese battling with *Margaux*.'

Leaving the dining-room again, he proclaimed, as if to convince himself, 'Not much wrong with a world where *Mersault* is followed by *Margaux*.'

'Howard really takes his job seriously, you know' Cindy said to Warne, 'despite his Steinway and his wines. He's not only head of department, he's also on all sorts of committees he needn't be on. He could give himself a much easier time.'

'It's one of the reasons I like him,' Warne said, 'because he doesn't. It's why Clarice liked him too.'

Margaux and cheese and another glass of water, and then it was time to go home to his empty house, walking the half hour short cut, some of it along a path through fields, most of it with the illuminated cathedral in view. Sometimes, when Clarice was alive, and they were looking forward to a walk with Howard and Cindy the next morning, they arranged to stay the night at Howard's. Stifling their giggles, they had drunken, comic sex in Howard's back bedroom. 'Hopeless. All that's happened is you've come all over me,' he could still hear Clarice protesting, as they both fell asleep.

Now, all he had were Cindy's parting kiss and hug.

In the city the cathedral offered itself as a beacon in the darkness.

'Can we be confident we've risen above such expressions of the human spirit?' Clarice once asked. 'Suppose we've fallen below them.'

'Or, are we always just the same?' he responded.

Always enemies, always people to be killed, so why not Clarice, Mark, Marina? Who could ever expect their time and place to be exempt from atrocity?

'You're not telling me everything,' he insisted to Pawsey this afternoon. 'What happened to Marina Scott after she handed the money back to Sewell?'

The end of a tour of Pawsey's prized, detached house, Pawsey revealing all the work he'd done on it over the years; extended kitchen, conservatory, *en-suite* bathroom.

'Everything for Barbara and the girls; doing all the plumbing, electrics, tiling, myself.'

The Met one world; his house another, a haven, separate; Sewell's bribes well spent.

All the daughters with post-graduate qualifications and impressive jobs: one a chemist for a major drug company, one climbing a ladder at Sky TV, the last, head-hunted in the IT world, working in the States, and married to a black lawyer, who was a former college offensive-tackle: 'Seven feet tall,' in Pawsey's words, 'and four feet wide, husband and bodyguard in Chicago.'

The battle with moles, 'Six fucking years till they just pissed off, had enough.'

Then, as they looked back admiringly from the end of the garden at the house, 'Barbara's mother died last year in Consett, County Durham. Ninety-three, same terrace house all her married life; two up, two down, bathroom squeezed into what used to be a pantry downstairs; lived in it seventy years; steel works saw her husband off in his sixties. When she died it had made her just over a thousand quid a year. This place is close to making more than that every week. Somebody tell me where the fucking justice is.'

Pawsey's bleeding heart.

Till on the landing, after all the traipsing about and then climbing the stairs, he suddenly collapsed onto a chair, gasping, 'Look at my fish.'

He meant the huge transparent tank, resting on an oak table under the stained glass landing window. In it, tiny, brilliantly coloured, tropical fish darted around, while bigger fish maintained a holding position, as if they knew they would never again have anywhere to go.

'Fucking lungs,' Pawsey wheezed desperately, almost weeping in his helplessness, 'fucking fags. They've killed me; Barbara, all this house, my daughters; a year, eighteen months, that's it.'

Towering over him, pressing down on his old man's shoulders, he demanded again, 'What happened to Marina Scott? I don't believe Sewell let her go once she'd returned the money. You're lying. She was responsible for his son's death. Tell me what happened, or, I swear, I'll break you and your fucking family, and your fucking house. You both knew she was Marilyn Scott's daughter. I bet you even knew the father.'

'Same name, same fucking hair as Marilyn's,' Pawsey gasped, helplessly. 'Yeah, we knew she was hers. Father? No idea. A fucking nut case; telling Maurice she'd work for him, better than his son; be a free agent, everything done professionally; no feelings, no morals, just do whatever he needed, totally committed. It was as if she was telling Maurice she could improve his fucking business.'

'What happened?'

'She'd been told to bring clothes, passport, everything.'

'And?'

'I left them to it, came home, knackered. I was supposed to be retired, out of it all. I wanted to get back to Barbara, this house, garden.'

'What happened to the girl?'

'She was going to a safe house Maurice had, near West Ham's football ground.'

'And?'

'She won't have left that house alive.'

19

He phoned Jane at seven in the morning.

'Tell me,' she urged, as soon as she recognised his voice.

'God, Jane, I'm so sorry. It's not good news. It's likely Marina's dead.'

'Oh no! Oh no!'

'Are you all right? Is there nobody around to help you? I wish I was with you.'

'Are you sure she's dead?'

'I can't be sure, but the man who told me had no reason to lie to me.'

'Oh, Marilyn and Marina, why?'

'Jane, are you going to be OK? Can you take a day off?'

'I don't want to be in the house on my own. I'll be better at work.'

'I've a big day in front of me, but I might be able to get a late train up to see you, then get back first thing. Can I stay with you?'

'You know you can.'

His doorbell rang. It would be Liz.

'Car's come for me, Jane. I'll phone later. For God's sake, look after yourself.'

Liz was driving him to the Edmondsons' house in Chilham. The squad for the search was assembling there at eight. Caroline Edmondson had provided keys to the house.

'I tracked Gillian's broker down on Saturday,' Liz said. 'He was at his golf club. He's phoning me back this morning.'

'Good. When we get to the house, you take a team upstairs. I'll do downstairs.'

'Anything else from Maidstone?'

'Sir Christopher's been on to Cunningham, asking if wasting police time isn't a crime. They've both got a national reporter lined up to smear us, assuming we find nothing.'

'Cunningham's supposed to be on our side.'

'He's only on his own side.'

The dirty white Focus with the dented wing was standing in front of the house, exactly where it had stood in February.

Addressing everybody, as Liz unlocked the house door, Warne said, 'You all know the score. We're looking for anything that might have a connection with the killing of Mark Farmwell-Pembury. Everybody in full search gear, evidence bags for anything we find. DS Ezeoke-Bruce's team upstairs, mine downstairs.

Always surreal searching through a house, uncovering peoples' lives, their secrets; happens to most people only when they're dead.

Helped by WPC Emily Graham, who'd driven him to the house a couple of months ago, he began in Gillian's meticulously arranged office, where the computer and other IT devices were already being bagged up. On one wall of shelves about sixty box files, finishing 1999-2000, faced them.

'Let's start with these, Emily,' he said. 'You at the right end. We'll meet in the middle.'

Forty-five minutes of invoices, receipts, letters, till WPC Graham exclaimed, 'Sir!'

On a desk she placed an open file, papers on the left on the lid, papers inside the box itself, but on top of these, resting on a white tea-towel, which WPC Graham had unwrapped, was a gun-metal paper-knife with an ornamental handle. Not a mark on it, it looked brand new.

'Wow! Well done, Emily. Go and get DS Ezeoke-Bruce. Don't say anything to anybody.'

Five minutes later Liz appeared, her phone to her ear,

'The broker,' she mouthed, then, into the phone, 'half a million Euros!'

Warne indicated the open box file on the desk. Walking over to it and seeing the paper-knife, she looked wide-eyed at Warne, before saying to the broker, 'We will certainly need an evidence statement from you, but I need to end this call now. I'll get back to you later this morning.'

'So that's the weapon,' she said.

'Looks like it. WPC Graham found it. Quick result.'

'Poor Gillian.'

She called in the photographers who were chatting in the hall.

'There's a smell of bleach from that box,' she said.

'Yeah. Gillian's used it to clean any blood stains off the knife.'

'But kept it. She could have thrown it away, anywhere.'

'It must have meant too much to her. If she killed Mark, I bet it wasn't planned. She's kept the knife for the record, like all the other stuff organised in those box files. She may have even wanted it to be found.'

'Something was planned. Her broker tells me he arranged half a million Euros for her. She had them some weeks before Mark's killing.'

'For the escape from her husband.'

'Escape to Europe, must be.'

Warne glanced at his watch, ten o'clock.

'I wonder how much of this search needs to go on, Liz. I'd say we make sure we're absolutely thorough with Gillian's office. There might be documents, letters. The safe needs to be opened.'

'They didn't keep much in the bedrooms, not even books. Upstairs it's like a hotel.'

'There's the garage and outbuildings, but what I'm thinking now is a press conference this afternoon, about three. There'll have to be a major hunt for Gillian, and if it's Europe it's Interpol.'

'So?'

'You finish up here. I'll get back to the station and organise things for this afternoon, when we'll both do the press conference.'

'Nobody more senior?'

'Who needs them!'

With the photographers finished, the box file, tea-towel, and paper-knife were bagged up. Warne had them placed in the boot of the car he would use, but just as he was about to slide behind the wheel his phone rang.

'Sergeant Stone here, sir.'

'Yeah?'

'We've got something in Selling, a couple of miles from you. Nobody else to deal with it.'

'What is it?'

'Looks like illegal immigrants, about a dozen girls for prostitution, held in a shipping container on a small-holding rented from the Farmwell-Penburys. A member of the public, training for the London Marathon, has jogged past it a couple of times and saw some of the girls yesterday, black and white. They weren't there the first time. They must have just arrived. They could disappear. A Lionel Chadwick rents the small-holding.'

Jesus, more Farmwell-Pembury!

'I'll see to it,' he said. 'Give me the directions. There's a maze of lanes around Selling.'

Back in the house he found Liz and explained. He selected WPC Graham, a DC and two PCs to accompany him; two cars in case of an arrest.

From the car he phoned Bob Burridge, Canterbury Gazette's chief reporter, asking Bob to contact the Nationals and TV about the press conference, sergeant Stone to confirm the arrangements. At least somebody's happy, he thought, as Bob's sense of importance ricocheted around his ear.

They drove down a narrow one-track lane that seemed to lead nowhere, but would eventually reach Selling. Hedgerows scraped the cars.

A worn-out cottage with a barn and other outbuildings to its right, empty space to its left. Behind it were a pick-up truck and the shipping container, with two stinking portaloos outside its entrance. Through the open doors Warne looked into its tunnel-like space, tables and benches filling the front end, bunk beds and mattresses the far end, where there was a solitary window. Along the right hand wall was a cold-water washbasin.

No girls, except for a beautiful black girl hanging washing on a line.

'We're police,' Warne announced. 'Where's Lionel Chadwick?'

The girl looked very scared.

'Take care of her Emily,' Warne said. 'The rest of you search the cottage.'

But a man, about thirty-five, in check-shirt and jeans, appeared at the cottage's back door.

'I'm Lionel Chadwick. You're fucking trespassing.' To the girl he said, 'Get inside, Diana.'

'We're police, and she's staying with us,' Warne said. 'How old is she, fourteen? Where's the other girls, who were here, living in that container?'

'What other girls?'

'We have a witness who's seen about a dozen girls here, black and white.'

'He's fucking lying.'

'We'll get forensics to look inside that shipping container, then we'll see who's lying.' To the two PCs he said, 'Cuff him. He's coming back to the station. Emily, stay with Diana, if that's her name. Come with me,' he said to the DC, 'we'll look around, starting with that barn.'

'It's locked,' Chadwick said, as the two PCs approached him..

'Where's the key? Come on. Hand it over. There's already a cell waiting for you.'

Sullenly, Chadwick produced keys from his pocket. Giving them to one of the PCs, he then held out his hands for the handcuffs.

Warne walked towards the barn with the DC. On their way was a heap of stuff, under black plastic sheeting, held down at its edges with bricks.

Warne lifted a corner of the sheeting.

'Hello, he said, 'here's the stolen lead from church roofs. Talk about a crime-scene. This place is becoming a whole bleeding drama.'

But nothing could have prepared him for what they found in the barn.

Under grey covers was a car, standing on blocks, its wheels removed.

Momentarily, he felt faint. He had to lean against the barn's door post.

'All right, sir?'

'My God. Gloves on, both of us.'

Lifting the covers from the bonnet and the boot, they folded them onto the roof.

The car was the dark blue Mark III Mondeo, the weapon that had killed Clarice. Spreading like a wound from beneath its left, smashed headlight back along the wing was a telling dent.

'Is this the car that killed your wife, sir,' the DC asked hesitantly.

'I'm sure it is.'

After lifting up the bonnet to reveal only the empty engine compartment, he walked slowly around the vehicle, as if it might have something to say to him, personally, about murdering Clarice. A Mondeo, after all, wasn't supposed to be a killing machine. It wasn't like some of the guns, and especially the knives, he'd seen, weapons looking like they had a life of their own, and might kill you of their own volition.

But only he broke the silence.

'Let's put the covers back on.'

Outside the barn he phoned Liz. She was just finishing at the Edmondsons' house.

'Get everybody over here, and we'll need more forensics. I'll arrange that.'

'What have you found?'

'It's a way-station for importing girls. We've got the lead from church roofs, and in the barn there's the Mondeo that killed Clarice.'

'No!'

'Yeah, I'm telling you.'

He phoned sergeant Stone to get some more people.

'I'm arranging the press conference,' Stone said.

'It's going to be a hell of a conference!'

Chadwick was standing handcuffed between the two PCs.

'That car in the barn,' Warne said to him.

'Some fucker was supposed to come for it.'

'If it was involved in a murder, you'll be an accessory.'

'Murder! You're fitting me up!'

'You're fitting yourself up.'

Liz and people from the Edmondsons' arrived, then more forensics.

He phoned Jane.

'It's a massive day. I won't make it tonight. We've found the car that killed Clarice.'

'Oh, poor you. Don't worry about me. If I need her, I can stay with my PA tonight, or she can stay with me.'

'I'll phone again as soon as I can.'

This is already becoming a relationship he was thinking, as Liz brought him back to Gillian Edmondson.

'I've spoken to Caroline, her daughter,' she said. Gillian speaks German. She spent six months in Berlin during her degree.'

'So that's where we get Interpol to make a start.'

'You do the press conference. I'll stay here,' Liz said.

'I want us both to do it. We'll postpone it till four. Some

of what we've found here will have to be yours, the car for a start. I can't be involved in that, but I do want to pursue the F-P connection. God knows how they're implicated in what's going on here.'

'I'd like the girls. Diana's from Benin City. She came with six other girls. Three were left in Paris. Her older sister was taken from here to London with about ten girls, mostly white. Chadwick kept Diana for himself. He keeps promising her she will be united with her sister. Another batch of about twelve girls left first thing this morning.'

'How old's Diana?'

'Not more than fifteen. I've arranged for social services to look after her. They'll pick her up from the station. Immigration will need to see her.'

Diana in one car, Chadwick in another, they drove back to the station.

Sergeant Stone greeted them.

'You're not gonna like this,' he said to Warne.

'What?'

'Maurice Sewell's done a runner.'

20

In Berlin's *Gemälde Galerie* Gillian Edmondson stood once more before Rembrandt's painting of his wife, Saskia, knowing she was unlikely to see the painting again for a long time. On this spot she had first met her lover, Angela Hartmann, a week after arriving in Berlin. Later today they were meeting at the Brandenburg Gate to walk the short distance to the British embassy in *Wilhelmstrasse*, where she would give herself up for the killing of her brother, Mark. Her written confession was in her handbag.

'If you prefer, I'll pick you up again in front of Saskia, as I did on our first day,' Angela joked this morning in her very good English. She had come into the bedroom for a kiss, as she left the flat in *Friedrichshain* to make her way to the *Fernsehturm* in *Alexanderplatz*. From there she was leading a Russian group on a guided Berlin walk, finishing at the Soviet War Memorial in the *Tiergarten*. Pulling on her clothes, Gillian smiled back sadly, remembering the cold, rainy, Tuesday afternoon over a month ago, in March, when Angela was suddenly by her side, as the two of them stood alone before Rembrandt's painting. Wanting to escape the weather, and with nowhere else to go, Gillian, for the first time in her life, had entered an art gallery, stopping before Saskia, because Saskia's face seemed full of sympathy.

'How Rembrandt honours her, so loving.'

Angela's first words.

Gillian silent in response, though registering the words

forever, as she began to wonder immediately where love and honour had been in her own life, and as she sensed, in Angela's presence, another revolutionary moment befalling her.

'It's the museum plan in your hand that tells me you're English,' Angela continued.

'Oh, I see.'

'The painting was begun before Saskia's death and finished afterwards. She died when she was thirty, after the birth of their son. It's probably why Rembrandt sees such vulnerability in her. None of their other three children survived.'

'Oh.'

'I'm sorry. Excuse me. I should be quiet and let you see the painting. I'm still being a guide. I've just finished a tour at the *Gedächtniskirche* with an English group. I always like to see Saskia. Rembrandt loved to dress her up for his paintings and, of course, he wanted to show everyone he could do the gold chain across her breast; also her pearl necklace, and the pearls on her ears and in her fur hat.'

'I have a daughter, Caroline. She's twenty-two, about to get married.'

Then she had begun to cry, silently and uncontrollably.

'Oh dear, do let me help you. Please, have these tissues. Would you like to take tea, or coffee, or something stronger.'

A brandy each in the gallery's café, Angela gazing at her very directly and asking, 'Are you as lonely as you look?'

The journey south-eastwards across Berlin to *Friederickshain*, for dinner and wine in Angela's flat.

Then, sex, without pain; at last; overwhelming.

Angela confessing later that night, as they lay blissfully together, 'It's the first time I've ever picked someone up, but I was so lonely myself, and you looked so stunning: short blond hair like a boy's, purple leather jacket, jeans, boots.'

'My disguise,' she replied, wondering why this kind of peace had never come earlier in her life; why she had never found it before her terrible deed. 'I had myself made-over the day after I reached Berlin. I discovered the hair is Annie Lennox's, because the hairdresser has her photograph in the window. I'm still not sure who Annie Lennox is. All my clothes are from a shop next door. I simply asked the girl there to dress me. I've thrown away all my other clothes. I've been back several times.'

Next day she left her aparthotel in *Potsdamer Platz*, moved in with Angela, and confessed everything to her; how it had happened that she killed her brother, Mark, when all she had ever intended was to entreat him to stay away from Dominic Mitcham, and not to break Caroline's heart.

'If you want us to have a future you need to give yourself up,' Angela declared, a week later, as they again lay together in the bedroom that used to belong to Angela's parents, and where Gillian always spent the night, snuggling up to Angela's soft plumpness. 'We used to live under the *Stasi*, so I know all about secret lives. They're a nightmare. Your hiding away won't work for us, even if you do have more Euros than I've ever seen in my life in that bag under the floorboards, where I occasionally hid my secret reading. You need to get straight with Caroline and the rest of your family, and the law.' Interlacing their fingers, she asserted determinedly, 'Our love for each other will see you through.'

In the gallery, Gillian now turned away from Saskia. She went to the café, where Angela had first taken her to comfort her.

With her *Kaffee und Kuchen*, she reviewed the course of her life over the past months, and her relationship with Angela. Fifty years old, Angela had been born and brought up in *Friedrichshain* when it was behind the Wall in the GDR, and when it was being re-built after Allied carpet-bombing. She lived in *Frankfurter Allee*, which used to be *Stalinallee*, in one of the 'workers' palaces'.

'Just after I was born,' she said, 'there was an uprising in the GDR against the government. It was begun by the construction workers building this accommodation and was finally suppressed by Soviet tanks. We got a very basic apartment, because my parents refused to be *Stasi* informers, and they found nothing to blackmail them with. Later, my lesbianism didn't help. Homosexuality was legalised in the GDR in 1968, a year earlier than in West Germany, but the *Stasi* took no notice. They still harassed my parents because of me.'

Garden of England to *Friederickshain*, Gillian reflected in the café; from a six-bedroom house in its own grounds to a cramped box of a flat looking down on a wide main road ('Perfect for tanks,' Angela said) and a railway bridge, not a tree in sight. When she was a student at the Free University of Berlin, she'd lived in the city's green southwest, in *Dahlem*. But Angela's flat would have been her paradise; if only.

Like her parents Angela was a schoolteacher. She taught Russian, English and History, until she retired ten years after the Wall came down, and began to get by as a Berlin guide.

'Strong from walking,' she said to Gillian, looking down at her legs as she slid her feet into her shoes, 'not very sexy. You have the legs of a model.'

'Your legs are sexy enough for me,' she replied, embracing Angela before resting her head on Angela's generous breasts, comforted again by a love almost motherly, but more intimate than ever a mother's love could be; finding the quick of her, as her husband had never even troubled himself to do.

'My parents bought the flat after Re-unification,' Angela told her, 'and almost immediately died, so it's mine. They smoked themselves to death calming their nerves. I still smell their cigarettes in the furniture and curtains. You too, I expect. It's one of the reasons I'm glad to walk the streets as a guide, though I haven't journeyed as far as my brother. He's in Santa Monica and wants nothing more to do with Germany. He's like one of my two other partners, who's now in Seattle.'

A week later, she said, 'Perhaps you can forget the past in America, and that's why President Bush thinks he'll have a blank page in Iraq.'

They were walking along an avenue of weeping birches in the Soviet war memorial at Treptower Park, a short distance from *Friederickshain*. Of the eighty-thousand Soviet soldiers dead from the battle of Berlin, Gillian learned seven thousand were commemorated here.

'Tomb of the Unknown Rapist,' Angela said. 'It's what women, my mother too, used to murmur about this place. My brother hated her saying it, but he never betrayed her. He only wanted to forget some of these soldiers might have killed our grandfather, who was defending the city against them, and raped our grandmother, till she attacked them with a kitchen knife and was shot dead. Memory, he believed, is always bad news for Germans.' Taking Gillian's hand and kissing her cheek, she sighed, 'I'm trying to learn from the past, but it's so difficult, when you've spent most of your life imprisoned in what was supposed to be an ideal.'

They were at the focal point of the cemetery, looking up at the colossal statue of a Soviet soldier securing a child aloft in his left hand, while the sword in his right impaled a dismembered swastika at his feet.

'St George and the dragon,' Angela said.

Irresistibly, Gillian saw again saw the paper-knife piercing Mark's chest.

What would she ever do with that memory?

'You're my third serious partner,' Angela told her on the way back to the flat. 'There's the one who left for America, and my first one, who discovered she wanted a man and a baby. So you see, I've been rejected twice, once for a man.'

'I wasn't entirely rejected,' Gillian remembered responding. 'It was more cruel. My husband didn't bother to hide from me that he was putting up with me only to promote his family's wine business. There was no physical wall, but I was a prisoner, and all of my family seemed to expect me to stay in my cell.'

Until she could no longer bear her husband's abuse.

'See a fucking gynaecologist and somebody for your head,' he gasped at her that last time, collapsing over her in their bed, after he had rammed his brutal penis, like a weapon, as deep into her as it could go. Always, penetrative sex had been torture for her, even more so after Caroline was born. Now, with Angela, learning to use gently, fingers, lips, tongue, she wondered if there was not always something in her head, something telling her body it was always wanting a woman, and not a man.

Carefully, she planned to desert her husband. Secretly her broker amassed Euros for her. All she had to do was pull her suitcase away from her husband's, as they approached the check-in at Heathrow, leaving him raging and helpless. Then smuggle herself away on a Eurolines bus to Berlin, where she'd spent six months as a student. There she would re-think her life.

Plans conceived before the horror of killing Mark.

In torment since Mark's Saturday evening birthday party, she waited nearly all of Sunday for her husband to leave for his regular liaison with Cambridge Katherine. Unable to contact Mark in what remained of the day, she walked to his house at three on the Monday morning, because she had to confront him. To save Caroline's marriage she had to break the relationship she had discovered between Mark and Dominic.

'All bases loaded,' a male guest at the party said to her, resignedly hitching his trousers above his swelling stomach, and coming down the stairs she was climbing to go to a bathroom. 'I'll find a tree in the garden.'

He obviously didn't know about the next flight of stairs to the second floor, where there were other bathrooms. These stairs were concealed behind a self-closing fire-door, barely distinguishable from the oak-panelling on the rest of the spacious landing.

Opening this door and climbing to the top of the house, she made her way to the furthest bathroom, only to hear, as she entered, from the bedroom next to it, muffled moans of sexual passion she identified as Dominic's, accompanied by Mark's seductively insinuating voice, 'There, there, you know you've always wanted it with me. I could always tell.'

Horrified, she ran from the bathroom, down all the stairs, and back into the thick of the party.

Caroline! Caroline! Caroline! Absent from the party; resting in her flat in Sevenoaks with a terrible migraine. How could her marriage go ahead?

At three in the morning she would bang on Mark's front door, so as to alarm him and catch him unprepared.

But surprisingly the door was only on the latch. The security lock hadn't been engaged, and there wasn't a sound from the alarm system.

Marching up the stairs to Mark's bedroom, she found a young man asleep and alone in Mark's bed; already, another conquest!

Maddened, she barged into the study, and grabbed the paper-knife from its stand for something to flourish, something to demonstrate how deadly serious she was.

Down the stairs she found Mark in the wet-room, standing under the beating jets of water.

'Gillian!'

Walking urgently towards her, sponge in hand, soap all over his body, he suddenly slipped on the wet tiles, fell towards her onto the upright paper-knife in her right hand, and, sighing 'Oh,' began to die immediately, his head over her right shoulder, the weight of his body pushing her over backwards, until she turned quickly to the left, pulling the paper-knife from his heart, as Mark smashed onto the floor.

Silence, except for the water hitting the tiles.

Cold numbness spreading all over her, as if she herself were entering death.

Blood spiralling under Mark's body.

Her brain, as always, reviving her, offering its calculations.

Go to the police, Dominic's relationship with Mark would have to be revealed. Marriage to Caroline was unlikely, if not impossible.

Conceal everything, Dominic could recover. Marriage to

Caroline could go ahead.

Beside her on the floor Mark lay dead, the lower half of his legs still in the shower area, his left hand beneath him as if to block the hole in his chest, his right arm stretched out above his head towards the wet-room entrance-door, the sponge on the floor and nearer the door.

Moving before the blood reached her, she picked up the sponge, and, backing out of the wet-room, carefully wiped every tile she had stood on, and finally, as she left, the door handle to the wet-room itself.

The only other thing she had touched with her hands was the latch on the entrance door to the house. Once in the house she'd marched everywhere like a soldier, up the stairs and into the bedroom and study, down the stairs and to the wet-room. Whatever traces she'd left, she might also have left at the party.

After wiping the door-latch with the sponge, she wiped the blade of the paper-knife, concealed sponge and paper-knife beneath her coat, and walked home in the darkness, already postponing, till after Mark's funeral, her plan to desert her husband.

'I'm very rich,' she said to Angela, showing her the bag of Euros. 'There's more where this came from, plus all my share of Farmwell-Pembury.'

Helping her conceal the bag beneath the floorboards in the smaller bedroom, Angela asked if all the money wasn't a burden.

'I never knew what to do with it,' she confessed. 'I convinced myself all was well, when the accounts were signed off, and my father's manoeuvrings concealed. Meeting you, I feel I've wasted most of my life. Events haven't touched me, as they've touched you. I paid no attention to them.'

'They've touched you now. A wall has come down for you too. Don't waste the rest of your life.'

'Recognise I'm gay, you mean. Reveal it to all my family.'

'Of course, and Caroline may have to recognise Dominic is gay.'

'It will break her heart.'

'No! Hearts are stronger than that.'

'You're rescuing me.'

'You just need help to rescue yourself. What you called your disguise really is you. You look lovely. You are lovely.'

'No-one else has ever said that to me.'

Humiliatingly, shamefully, she knew now she had been so wrong to be contemptuous of Mark's homosexuality. Abnegation had made her self-righteous and resistant to self-knowledge; oblivious to any connection with a world larger than Farmwell-Pembury enterprises.

Guiltily, she saw ultimate, murderous, annihilating, self-righteousness, when Angela took her, on a freezing day, to *Sachsenhausen*, the concentration and extermination camp just north of Berlin.

On the parade-ground, as the icy cold assaulted them, she imagined standing there in pyjama-like clothes. Later, in one of the buildings, she saw a device on which a prisoner would be commanded to stand naked in order to be weighed and measured. Behind the prisoner a little panel could be slid to one side, so the prisoner could be shot in the back of the head.

A fortnight later Angela returned to the flat, at the end of the afternoon, with a *Daily Mirrror* given to her by a member of an English group she had been guiding. Half the front page displayed a photo of Gillian Edmondson, wanted in connection with the death of her brother, Mark Farmwell-Pembury. According to the report, the weapon that killed Mark had been found, and Interpol was searching for Gillian Edmondson in Berlin.

'They might not find you using this photo,' Angela said. 'You now look ten years younger. But they'll find you eventually. Make it easier for yourself and us. Give yourself up.'

'I always expected the paper-knife to be found,' she said. Then, as if to distract, 'The photo's an old one. I was persuaded to do a publicity shot.'

'Don't be afraid,' Angela embraced her and kissed her closed eyelids. 'I'll always love you, and I'll wait for you, if I have to. At *Sachsenhausen* you saw what it is to *want* to kill, and that is not you. You killed your brother in an accident, and that will be your defence.'

Most of her life Angela had known fear.

'When were thirteen,' she said, 'we were brought from school to stand on the Wall near the Brandenburg Gate. West Germans waived at us, but we kept our hands by our sides. We were too frightened to waive back.'

21

Where the fuck was Sewell? If he had him, Warne was sure he could nail him for killing Clarice. To escape complicity in murder, Lionel Chadwick was singing. Yeah, the girls were Sewell's business and so was the Mondeo. No, he'd never seen the driver before or since. 'Be sure to hide this fucker. Somebody'll move it on,' was all the driver said, as he got out of the Mondeo and straight into a waiting Transit. Nobody coming for the Mondeo, Chadwick began to dismantle it, taking parts to the scrapyard near Dartford, where he also transported the lead, supplied to him by a small-time local gang, nothing to do with Sewell.

Stupid bastard should shut up, Warne thought. Sewell would look after him inside. Inside after singing, Sewell will have him broken apart.

'No members of the Farmwell-Pembury family were personally involved in renting out that small-holding near Selling,' the F-P solicitor had declared authoritatively on TV news. 'Along with other pieces of land it's been rented out through an agency to various tenants for over fifty years. The family had no knowledge of what was happening during the tenancy of Lionel Chadwick, or of Lionel Chadwick's alleged connections to the criminal, Maurice Sewell. It has now removed all its business from the hands of the agency that arranged this tenancy.'

F-Ps always concealed behind their screens, Warne said to himself, stoking his anger further by rehearsing the farce of

Sewell's escape.

Re-designated a cat. B prisoner, and his priest pleading he be allowed to visit his dying mother in her luxurious nursing home in Folkestone; all the fire-alarms going off after he held her hand for half an hour; several men in white coats bursting into the bedroom to hustle Sewell, and the officer he was handcuffed to, out of the building and into a waiting van; TV cameras the first to find the van, burnt-out down a country lane, with the officer hooded, and handcuffed to a tree.

'Carry on Criminals!'

If it's not on TV, it's not happening.

He and Liz had been all over TV themselves; arriving at Gatwick at the weekend with the handcuffed Gillian Edmondson. Already there were 'before' and 'after' photos of Gillian dominating the media. 'Before' was the drab, don't-look-at-me accountant displayed during the 'woman-hunt.' 'After,' with her short-cropped bleached hair, jeans and biker's leather jacket, was what one tabloid hailed as 'the power of love,' meaning the power of lesbian sex with Angela Hartmann.

And over a week ago, on May Day, Bush himself had performed for the world's screens like a regular Hollywood hero. In full pilot's kit, trusty helmet under his arm, as if returning at least from a moon-shot, he'd stepped down from a navy fighter-jet aboard the aircraft carrier USS Abraham Lincoln, a banner high over his right shoulder triumphantly proclaiming, 'Mission Accomplished'.

Were Liz and me putting on a show, Warne asked himself; feeding a ravenous public; offering to its appetites the daughter of Sir Christopher and Lady Farmwell-Pembury, no less; the sensational killer of her gay brother, because he was seducing her daughter's fiancé; now gay herself and arriving at Gatwick with her German, ex-communist, female lover, and being transformed immediately into a gay icon?

Soaps couldn't compete!

The more he understood Gillian, the greater the distance between her reality and the scenes he was compelled to enact; so much so, that had it been down to him, he would simply have recorded the events leading to Mark Farmwell-Pembury's death, and then left Gillian and Angela Hartmann to live in Berlin in peace.

But it was at least one mission accomplished. Mark's killer had been captured.

As for the Bush episode, forget reality! With the carrier anchored thirty miles off the San Diego coast, Bush could easily have been chauffeured onto it in the presidential helicopter.

'Remember,' Howard said on the phone last night, 'America can be as much movie-land as real-land. They *did* have to invent what was going to happen in that new world.'

Maybe Bush had no doubts about what had been staged for him. On the first of May, he might actually have believed 'Mission Accomplished,' even though American generals said thousands of soldiers would still be needed to secure Iraq's thousands of miles of inhospitable territory and the vast piles of weapons lying around in military areas.

'The President of the USA needs to present himself as writing the script,' Howard added, 'even when all of history, 9/11 included, shows events write an elusive script of their own.'

Too true; this Friday morning, while Warne was having his breakfast, the script reported on the radio that Captain Dominic Mitcham had been killed on the outskirts of Basra by a roadside bomb. He was in one of the lightly armoured 'snatch' Land Rovers soldiers named 'mobile coffins,' the attack happening two days before Bush's speech.

Overwhelming for Caroline Edmondson, Warne thought. Already she's devastated by her mother's confession, and the confirmation that Dominic might be gay. Her mother's own gayness barely seemed to register on her.

He'd allowed Gillian to see Caroline immediately. Always Gillian stuck to the statement she had written out in Berlin. It recounted what she discovered about Mark and Dominic on the night of Mark's birthday party, and why she went to Mark's house in the Monday morning darkness. It told how Mark had slipped and fallen onto the paper-knife. Crucially, for the likely defence, it was supported by Caroline's tearful confession that she had herself queried Dominic's sexuality. In support of her mother, she promised to try to persuade Dominic to admit to what had happened at Mark's party, and to acknowledge his bi-sexuality, if not his homosexuality.

'Why wasn't it the terrible stress of this Iraq war?' she insisted. I'll always love him. If he wants me, I'll still marry him.'

'So you should, my love?' Gillian said, embracing her.

But with Dominic dead, where will the defence go now, Warne wondered. Dominic's parents were conservative Christians; unlikely, therefore, to acknowledge any homosexual tendencies on his part, especially as the prosecution would obviously dismiss them as a defence invention.

Liz's report on developments from the small-holding near Selling was on his desk. She'd organised the forensic match of the damage to the Mondeo with the damage to his motorbike, stored in his garage. The young woman, Diana, who was pregnant with Chadwick's child, was now in a charitable safe-house, but there was no trace of her sister.

This afternoon Danny Barratt, the student picked up in Dover by Mark the night he was killed, was due back at the station with his father.

'Gillian's absolutely certain,' Liz said, after they'd been through the bail proceedings for her, 'that the door to Mark's house wasn't locked, when she pressed its handle down in the middle of the night. She wouldn't have got in otherwise, because she never had a key.'

'And she says the alarm system was switched off,' he added. 'Knowing about Mark's expensive security-lock, she'd expected to bang hard on the door to waken him up. That was part of her plan to shock him.'

'So why was the alarm off, and the door only on the latch?'

Danny Barratt must know.

He likes living on the edge and over it, Warne thought.

One-night-stands, another performance; like that woman with me twenty-odd years ago.

And now?

He'd spent a weekend with Jane, most of it in her bed, because they couldn't have enough of each other.

'You might not believe this,' she sighed, as they both again returned to the world. 'I've been nearly a virgin for twenty years.'

'Me too, since Clarice died.'

'I'll never mind you speaking of her.'

'I can't forget her, but I need another life.'

'With me?'

'Yeah.'

'Oh that makes me so happy. I saw your love for Clarice. I've waited all my life to have love like that come my way.'

He believed her, because any man looking at her could see she could have sex any time she wanted it. Like Clarice, Jane was a serious woman, but a different kind of serious woman, belonging more to the day to day world. All the odds against her as a single mother, she'd handled life as she found it and succeeded in it. During the weekend, on the Saturday morning, a call came from a plumber complaining he hadn't been given enough time for the job he was on.

'We went through the time and costings together, Bob,' she responded firmly. 'I'm not going to ask the customer to pay more. That way we lose business, because people don't trust us. If it takes you longer, it's your own time and money.'

'A new bathroom suite,' she reported to Warne. 'He can fit it in his sleep. He's trying it on.'

Jane ready to transform her life and be with him! What a compliment!

'Don't let her down,' he told himself, looking into the mirror this morning, then packing his bag in readiness for another weekend with her straight from work; also see aunty Lucy, his mother's sister, and watch United, already champions, play Everton at Goodison Park.

Hadn't he had enough of sorrow?

'*When sorrows come, they come not single spies, / But in battalions.*'

That was the F-P solicitor at Nystole, when they were all there to confirm the arrangements for bringing Gillian from Berlin. Dominic Mitcham was still alive. As usual, Sir Christopher and Lady Penelope were admirably costumed.

'*Hamlet*,' the solicitor added, as if to get everyone on

common ground.

'I know where the lines are from,' Sir Christopher responded derisively.

Because you're a fucking Claudius, Hamlet's uncle, Warne suddenly thought, as he took a seat alongside Liz on one of the wine-coloured chesterfields. He remembered Clarice saying Claudius on stage should always look the part of a king, even though he was a murderer.

'How do we know my daughter's confession, delivered into the British embassy in Berlin is true?' Sir Christopher challenged. 'How do we know she is in her right state of mind?'

'It was written down in advance and freely given,' Warne replied. 'And she also describes the part played by the paper-knife, which must be the one we found in her office at her house.'

'Too horrible, too horrible,' Lady Penelope said, her voice breaking.

Ignoring her, Sir Christopher confronted what he wanted the world to see as self-evidently preposterous.

'My family is to face the trial of my daughter for the murder of my son, and both my son and daughter are being revealed to be homosexuals!'

'We must hope for manslaughter, and perhaps even then not guilty,' the solicitor offered.

'Ever since the last war, people in this country have schemed to bring our kind of people down,' Sir Christopher countered aggressively.

'I don't think bail for your daughter will be opposed,' Warne said, looking at a stricken Lady Penelope.

'We must do everything we can to comfort her, and Caroline,' she responded, looking gratefully at Warne. 'And we ourselves must be consoled by Gillian at last finding someone to love. It's a tragedy for her that it has only happened because of a terrible accident.'

'Someone to love!' Sir Christopher exclaimed, contemptuously.

'Of course, how can you think otherwise? We both know Gillian was imprisoned in an unhappy marriage. We have not been successful parents to either of our children.'

'*We* are not the issue,' Sir Christopher proclaimed, venting his fury into the empty spaces of the room. '*We* are not to be questioned.'

You will be, you bastard, Warne thought.

22

Danny Barratt, with a strong, full beard, looked older than two months ago; more confident, even cynical.

'OK, I fixed the door and the alarm, so what?' he finally asserted.

'So what! You know so what,' Warne said. 'Gillian Edmondson only got into the house, because the door was on the latch. Had it been locked, she'd have had to disturb Mark, as she planned, and he'd still be alive.'

'His death's not down to me.'

'Why did you unlock the door and switch-off the alarm?'

'Because you never know.'

'Never know!'

'About the guy; suppose he's a freak. You might have to get the hell out.'

'Danny!' his father pleaded. 'What are you saying? What kind of world do you live in?'

'Dad!' the son responded, tears threatening his eyes. 'You and mum, what do you know? Same every day and night for thirty years.' He paused, repressing his tears, before insisting, 'A stranger's bedroom in a strange place! You look after yourself, make sure you can be out of there.' Turning to Warne, he explained, 'That's the real reason for the cut-throat you found in my shaving things. There's been times I've threatened to use it. So now, I always think ahead. While Mark was in the *en-suite*, I went downstairs, unlocked the door, and cancelled the alarm.

I knew the code, because I stood by Mark while he tapped it in. He told me the numbers were the first four of his birthday, 16-2-5, and said a night with me would be "a late present". When he came out of the *en-suite*, I was already in the bed.'

'Why didn't you say all this in your first statement?' Warne demanded.

'Guilt. I wanted to push guilt away. Mark was as good a one-night as you'll ever have. He was only looking for pleasure, and so was I; coffee and *croissants* in the morning the only consequence. His death *is* down to me.'

'You didn't tell us the truth,' Warne responded angrily. 'You wasted our time searching for a key. That's perverting the course of justice.'

'Oh, no!' from Danny's father.

'Oh, yeah,' from Warne, as he signalled the meeting was at an end. 'We'll need another formal statement. Danny can make it later to DS Ozeoke-Bruce.'

'I'll drive you to the station before taking Danny's statement,' Liz said to him, when they were alone in his office. 'I see you've got your bags packed.'

'Bag,' he replied.

'Go now, before anything else turns up.'

'I'm just about to go, but I can walk through town to the West Station. I'm going to have a pint at the Westgate before I get on the train'

'I'll drive you to the Westgate. Start relaxing now. Give yourself a good time. You deserve it,'

'Aren't I supposed to give the orders around here?'

'I said start relaxing.'

Which he did, snoozing all the way to London after his pint, and snoozing some more, after another pint in the city, first class all the way to Manchester Piccadilly.

'Suppose he's a freak,' he heard Danny Barratt say again, when he was on the Manchester train; 'a stranger's bedroom in a strange place.'

Only happened to him once, because he'd fallen in love with Clarice so early; both of them losing their virginity to each other during the first year at university; Clarice limiting their meetings in the last year; joking she was getting herself 'to a nunnery' to prepare for finals.

Crazy literature she read; weird lives he mingled with; every kind of sex available; entirely conventional themselves.

Just one Danny Barratt moment, when he was a student; that Justine, still with him, after more than twenty years; he'd fuck her better now.

'Why don't you dance with me?'

Final year, February; writing an essay all Saturday; sinking pints in the Students Union at nine o'clock, aching for sex with Clarice; watching the dancers and listening to that great blues band, especially the singer; still see the singer; black window-cleaner from Hunslet, sounding like he'd lived all his life on the Mississippi Delta.

'*Gimme Some Lovin'*.'

'Come on. Dance with me.'

About twenty-eight, tall, strongly built, short dark hair, tight dress, tits in your face.

Seizing his hand and pulling him onto the floor.

'I'm Justine.'

'David.'

'You like this music?'

'Yeah, the singer's doing Freddie King. My flatmate has the CD. Eric Clapton's a fan.'

'You're a student?'

'Yeah, final year, you?'

'No chance; work in a bank.'

Amazonian, great body.

Buying him a drink, when the song came to an end.

'I'm sure I've more money than you.'

Pint for him, double vodka for her; wallet stuffed with notes; band into *Love in Vain*.

'Great Robert Johnson blues,' he said. 'Mick Jagger's done it. Robert Johnson's supposed to have sold his soul to the devil.'

'Really?'

But she wasn't interested.

'What do you do in your bank?'

'Back-rooms, where all the decisions are made; all men, but a bunch of old women really. I'm going to pass every banking exam in sight and climb over the lot of them.'

'Ambitious.'

'Why not? And you?'

'I'm thinking of the police, when I graduate.'

Standing back to size him up.

'You'll make a very strong arm of the law.'

Singer back to Freddie King, as they finished their drinks.

'*Help me through the day; help me through the night.*'

Pulling him onto the floor and wrapping herself around him.

Couldn't stop his erection; didn't want to.

In the darkness, her right hand sliding down his body to squeeze his dick.

'What do we have here? It's not just the singer asking for

sweet loving. Come on, now, my place.'

'Wha …? My coat.'

'Get it tomorrow.'

A BMW 3 Series in the car park; a new town-house in north Leeds.

'Upstairs to the top floor. Use the front bedroom and the *en-suite*. Wait for me.'

Telling himself it was, 'Just a shag. Any minute, nearly all that dance floor will be shagging. Clarice will never know.'

Sitting on the bed in his boxer shorts.

'Good, you're ready.'

Pushing him onto his back, removing his shorts.

'Now there's a policeman's helmet!'

Expertly arousing him further; ignoring his hands on her bare breasts.

Looking ready to throw a javelin, when she stood up to let her robe fall from her.

Sheathing him with a condom; pinning his hands above his head, as she mounted him.

Helplessly realising *she* was shagging him; praying he would last long enough for her.

Convulsive heaves and shrieks, as she came, collapsing down on him, her breasts smothering his face, his own feeble thrill lost in her powerful, shuddering, climax.

Silently lying beneath her body, so much heavier than Clarice's, till she slid off him.

'What do you want to do now? You can stay in the next bedroom till morning, or leave.'

'Leave, now!'

'We've had sex. That's all I wanted. All you wanted. I like my bed to myself, when it's all over. It was very good, by the way.'

'You got yours, all right.'

'Isn't that what it's all about, getting what we want? You surely didn't think I was offering you more than a fuck. Christ, don't tell me you're like all the men I work with; no idea of women as anything other than housewives. You should hear some of the girls I have in this bed.'

'Girls!'

'Why not? You think only men can give pleasure to women. I've had women in this bed who've never had an orgasm from men pumping into them. They're so grateful, do anything.'

'And when it's all over?'

'They usually spend the night in the next bedroom. They're always gone when I wake up. Considering their position, I suppose.'

'I'm going now.'

'Suit yourself. If we ever see each other again, don't even offer to recognise me.'

At Piccadilly station, on the platform, Jane kissed him passionately on the lips.

23

Next morning, Jane's warm softness lingering all over him, it was aunty Lucy whose cheek was against his, her arms around him.

'David, love,' she said.

Hardly anything of her, but always full of tension he thought, taking the easy chair by her bedside. Handing her one of the cups of tea provided by Annie, her youngest daughter, who was downstairs, he glanced at the black and white photos on the cabinet at the other side of the bed. One was of uncle Jack as a young man, his shirt opened at the neck over the collar of his jacket. By its side was the wedding photo after the war; his aunty, girl-like, in a white bridal dress 'everybody saved coupons for'; his uncle, dead now for six years, in his Eighth Army uniform.

Warne had arrived by bus at half-past ten, getting off at Lovers' Lane, where his aunty had lived for over fifty years. Later, he would walk through Atherstone to get a bus back to Jane's from the other end of town. On the phone from Canterbury he'd told his aunty he'd become friends with Jane Scott and would would be staying with her. 'Oh!' she responded ambiguously, knowing what nearly everybody knew about Marilyn Scott.

'You're keeping as well as can be expected?' she now asked, sipping her tea.

'That's about right.'

'What you've been through.'

'I've had my share.'

Her white face stared grimly towards the foot of the bed. A good husband, four daughters, a comfortable house, it was as if life had let her down, and she couldn't forgive it. What had happened to Clarice and himself would only have been more evidence for her case.

'Your uncle Jack deserves a win on't pools for livin' with your aunty Lucy,' his dad used to reflect triumphantly, when the two of them were alone together.

'What do you think of Atherstone, when you come back to it?' she asked.

'I've not seen much of it.'

'Steel shutters on all the shops at night, even the undertaker's, where I'll be going soon; as if people want to steal dead bodies, like savages!'

'We don't have these shutters in the middle of Canterbury, but there's enough crime there too.'

'Hmm.'

Her angina could take her any time, he thought, remembering aunty Lucy and uncle Jack had always treated him as a kind of son, causing jealousy, combined with political antagonism, in his dad, who worked in overalls and voted Labour, while uncle Jack, who'd advanced from the factory floor to become a buyer for Prospero's, wore a suit and tie all day and was on the committee of Atherstone's Conservative Club.

But he could never persuade his wife and Warne's mother even to go near a polling station, let alone vote Conservative.

'You'll never vote Labour, so why not vote for us?' he pleaded. 'What have we done wrong?'

What he must have done right, Warne surmised, was take off his suit and tie and lie all night with aunty Lucy in Lovers' Lane, overcoming that apparent distrust of pleasure in her, which monotonously inspired the mockery of her four sons-in-law. Vividly he remembered an episode when he was eight and was at his aunty's with his mother, who was having tea with three or four other women. Lying on the floor, playing with a toy car and glancing up the skirts of the women, he was oblivious to what they were saying, until one of them announced, 'No man has ever seen me with no clothes on.'

'Well, you don't know what you've missed,' his aunty responded derisively, glancing guardedly at his mother, who belatedly joined in the laughter of the other women.

'Next door's been sold for buy-to-let,' she said passing Warne her empty cup. 'Pakistani landlord, Pakistani tenants. It'll happen to our house, when I'm gone. Annie says these Pakistanis always pay good money, so how can you turn them down?'

He didn't reply, 'Would you want to?' He knew that when aunty Lucy and Uncle Jack moved into Lovers' Lane, Pakistani neighbours would have seemed as likely as neighbours from the moon. Instead he said, 'Ordinary people can find it difficult to buy a house nowadays, and getting a council house is next to impossible, thanks to Maggie selling them off, and Blair.'

'Hmm,' she said again, as if he'd missed the point. 'I'd never have married your uncle Jack, if he'd only offered me a council house.'

When he let this go, she continued, 'I wouldn't care, but nobody, black, brown, or white wants a front garden any more. Everything's paved over for cars. Your uncle Jack loved his lawn and his roses.'

And she, Warne knew, had loved Lovers' Lane, so much so she'd been its self-appointed warden for several years after her retirement. She'd required other residents to pick up litter in front of their houses and told them when they put out the wrong wheelie bins for emptying. But gradually her authority diminished, as former neighbours disappeared, and she was only the old lady marooned and waiting to die at number twenty-four. Before her retirement she'd been a receptionist in a doctor's surgery, where, Warne's mother told him, some patients claimed she delivered the most useful diagnoses. 'A sword and a shield,' the male head of the expanded practice joked about her, when she retired.

Angina or no angina, she looks as though she'd like to put somebody to the sword this morning, Warne thought. Something's raging inside her.

'You've solved your crime,' she said.

'About time, but it mainly solved itself.'

'Poor woman.'

'Poor woman?'

'Who had to run away to Germany.'

'Oh, Gillian Edmondson. I'm hoping she'll have a happy ending, eventually.'

'The papers say her husband's disowning her, and her father wants nothing more to do with her.'

'Her mother's moved in with her and the German woman.'

'While the men go Scot-free.'

'It suits them both to have it put out there's a streak of craziness in Gillian that's breaking up the family, but I hope the trial will dispense with that. All Gillian wanted was to love a partner who would love her.'

Silence from aunty Lucy. Who knew what she thought of lesbianism?

But then she declared, passionately, 'Men can be monsters towards women.'

'Aunty?'

Abandoning the pillows' support, as if to demonstrate she would never settle for helplessness, she sat upright, looking ready for a decisive testament.

'I asked you to come all this way to see me, because there's something you need to know. When I'm dead, you and two other women in Atherstone will be the only people who know, apart from Charles Farmwell-Pembury. We want revenge.'

'Charles Farmwell-Pembury? Revenge? For what? Know about what?'

'About your mum, her breakdown, when she was nineteen.'

'That! I never want to think about it anymore. All my life in Atherstone I heard people say it was an excuse for not working, even in an office. They said that photo in Billy Lee's window, comparing my mother to Ava Gardener, went to her head. She thought too much of herself to get up every morning like everybody else and work for a living.'

Resisting tears, he pronounced for his aunty and himself the well-known advertisement:

BILLY LEE PHOTOGRAPHER
KEEPING YOUR HAPPY MEMORIES ALIVE

Clarice and he used to gaze at the latest weddings, christenings, public presentations, in his studio display window. By then Billy Lee's photograph of his mother, at eighteen, alongside a Hollywood publicity shot of Ava Gardener, had long been removed.

'Oh, Jean, love,' his aunty broke out sobbing. 'You were so beautiful, not like me.'

'Aunty!'

'She was never frightened of work, me neither.'

'What happened?'

'She was assaulted.'

'Assaulted?'

'Sexually assaulted, by Christopher Farmwell-Pembury, after the war, when he was at Prospero's, before he married and moved to Kent.'

'What! What are you saying? He raped her!'

'He used to ask her to stay late in the offices, do some special work for him, for extra pay, good money. It went on for a few weeks. Then he trapped her in a room at the back, where he asked her to search through some old files.'

'You *are* saying he raped her!'

'It was terrible. She was a virgin, engaged to that Geoffrey Carswell, who became a solicitor. The coward asked for his ring back, when your mum became ill. There was only me in the house, when she got home. Our mum and dad were at the pictures. She was in a dreadful state. Her blouse and underclothes were ripped. She was still bleeding. We hid everything away till we burned it. Our mum and dad never knew what happened. Nobody did. Our Jean was lucky she wasn't pregnant.'

'You didn't go to the police?'

'Against the Farmwell-Pemburys, and him with his war

record! They had their own way in everything in this town. Your uncle Jack and me were just about to get married ourselves. We'd all have been humiliated. It was bad enough, when your dad discovered our Jean wasn't a virgin, though he never knew why.'

'Bastards! Bastards!' They ruined her life!'

'Shush. Sit down again, David love. Don't let Annie hear you.'

'There'll be more than Annie will hear me! Oh, that bastard!'

His aunty gestured for a tissue. She also pointed to the drawer in the bedside cabinet at his side of the bed. 'There's an envelope for you in that drawer.'

Struggling to become calm, he opened the drawer and took out an A4 envelope, one of the thicker, stronger kind, fastened with a string. His name was hand-written on it. Inside he felt papers and some soft material.

'Two more women's details in there, widows, still alive. They were assaulted too, after they were married, but their marriages stayed together, because their husbands thought it was something they'd done, without knowing what they were doing. I remember the wives coming to the surgery. I'd not been there long myself. It was over about eighteen months, first one, then the other, bleeding like your mum. The doctor had one of the husbands in for a talking to, telling him he shouldn't do that to his wife. There was nearly a fight in the surgery. But I always knew about our Jean, and I've been talking to the two other women. They've nothing to lose now, so they're not frightened of speaking up for themselves. They can't wait to testify against a monster like Christopher Farmwell-Pembury. We want him exposed and imprisoned before he dies, and we die. Inside that big envelope there's another opened envelope with ten pounds in it. It's what he used to give the women afterwards. Your mother never touched her envelope. She left it with him, but Polly Aldred's kept hers with the notes inside all these years. His finger-prints will be on everything. And she's kept her torn knickers too. They're in the tissue paper. Some of her blood and his stuff's still on them. You'll be able to use it for what-do-you-call-it?'

'DNA.'

24

'A present for you too, David, love,' Annie said, nodding at the envelope, before they kissed each other, as he left aunty Lucy's. 'Mum gives everybody something to remember her by.'

Not like this, he thought, wanting to smash Sir Christopher Farmwell-Pembury's face in. That knight of the fucking realm raping my mother, breaking her for the rest of her life, and likely courting his future wife at the same time.

And next to no chance of a historical rape conviction, even if DNA offered anything. Polly Aldred must be near eighty. In court against the kind of barrister the Farmwell-Somburys would employ, and facing an accusation of offering herself to Christopher Farmwell-Pembury as to a film star, she'd be destroyed.

What a fucking family of exploiters; screwing young women workers at Prospero's like plantation owners with their slaves; Mark a predator just like his father. And Lady Penelope, charming people her husband was screwing.

Charming me!

'Bastards!' he said again out loud in futile relief for his pain.

All around him now was Atherstone's decaying town centre, as exploited and demeaned as its workers had been and still were, the future thanklessly discarding it for the supermarkets and superstores on the bypasses; New Labour leaving it to its fate. Defiantly, a few small businesses made a stand, like the undertakers aunty Lucy was destined for. As if immune to any destiny, it and a hair and beauty salon still shared the same building, the salon's customers separated from the dead in their coffins only by the wall of mirrors they gazed into.

That double-barrelled bastard must have always had his notes ready.

'Here, pull yourself together. There's ten pounds in there, a lot of money. Treat yourself. You enjoyed it. Women always do.'

Treating my mother as a whore, and Carswell in on it too, I bet; offering his future wife as a down payment for Farmwell-Pemburys favours. No wonder my mother nearly lost her mind completely, especially when Carswell saw how destroyed she was and asked for his ring back. And later she meets him with his replacement wife and kids; descending from his big detached house up the hill near the Farmwell-Pembury place. I used to see him too, with his youngest child. Just let me run into him now!

And you, Sir Christopher Farmwell-Pembury, I'll crucify you; you and Maurice Sewell both.

'Remember Jean Roberts? You raped her in a store-room at Prospero's in 1947, when she was just nineteen. She was my mother. You raped other women at Prospero's, and you've raped since, I bet. That's why you don't want your DNA on file.'

Walking past Prospero's, he looked into its rubbish-filled entrance court-yard, commercial space advertised on all floors, ornamental urns from the double staircase, and stained-glass from the main office windows, long gone. Even on a Saturday morning everything was closed up, so he couldn't flash his warrant card and search out that store room.

Vulnerable young women and a powerful male boss, chest

full of medals as a war hero; one of the cunts who would always claim to have 'served,' and would always be acknowledged to have 'served,' in a way that was said of all sorts of people in governing positions, starting with the fucking royal family, but never of the working-class, except in a menial capacity. Clarice hated this set-up, hated any complicity in it. That last time they were in Manchester four years ago, on their way to some walking in the Yorkshire Dales, and so he could watch United play Leeds.

In Chetham's Library, facing each other across the table in the window, where Marx and Engels had faced each other in the summer of 1845.

'Peterloo Massacre, Emmeline Pankhurst, radical protest,' she said. 'For real Labour politics we should have stayed up here, in Manchester. Your football team is here. Fergie supports Labour.'

'No more radical protest in Manchester nowadays than anywhere else, and we wanted to experience London.'

'I know; theatre, galleries, museums. But then we moved to Kent.'

'It was a good opportunity for us both. We still had London, and France was even nearer.'

'All true, but it's made us too accepting of the way things are. Everything about our lives moves us further and further away from the working class.'

'Blair's always realised he's got to persuade Tories to vote Labour and there's only so much socialism they'll take. We've got to recognise that too.'

'New Labour! Mrs Thatcher says it's her greatest achievement.'

When he didn't reply, she went on, 'Blair wants to take class out of politics, but we both know it's always there. Look at that Hillsborough football disaster he's refusing to investigate. Nearly a hundred lives lost from a Labour city, and it's as if they don't count, because they're labelled football hooligans, working-class and dispensable, like the miners under Thatcher.'

'Blair's supposed to be a football fan, Newcastle United.'

But aware his words were a distraction from his shame over the police's handling of Hillsborough, she stood up saying, 'If Labour forgets the working-class, the working-class will forget Labour. They'll find somewhere else to go, and Labour might as well pack it in.'

He was entering lines of terrace houses built at right angles to Prospero's. Stepping out of these houses, you must have felt the cotton-mill was your destiny; either that, or turn the other way to walk through the fields, perhaps to be a farm-labourer or, much more likely, a miner in the Farmwell-Pembury, then National Coal Board, mines, whose winding-gear you could see from the end of the street, and whose sirens, beginning and ending the shifts, told you the time more reliably than any clock or watch you owned. Now these coal-mines were as defunct as Prospero's, obliterated by Thatcher and Major after the defeat of the miners, their only product nostalgia. On TV Warne had seen university educated Labour politicians trying not to forget the working class, as they sentimentalised a brutal industry, in which they would never have encouraged their own children to work.

Soon he was in one of 'the backs,' separating the tiny yards of lines of terrace houses. Coming home from school along this alley-way, he often saw, through the open gate to her back-yard, Clarice Pomeroy, who worked early in the mornings delivering milk. She would be in her painter's overalls, kneeling by the side of her BSA 250, an oily rag or a spanner in her hand, and, between her lips, one of the cigarettes that killed her. Always, after his relationship with Clarice began, she gave him a slight, knowing smile.

'What do your mother and Clarice Pomeroy do on their motor-bike trips together?' he said to Clarice when they were seventeen.

'I don't know. Why don't you ask them?'

At the end of the alley-way was a lane at right-angles. Across this were semi-detached houses built in the thirties, with drives and gardens. The first of these had been bought by 'Flagger Bill' for his beautiful new, damaged, bride.

'When your dad sang *Comfort ye* from *Messiah,* it was as if he was singing it only for your mum,' aunty Lucy told him, when he was preparing to leave for university. 'She was standing in the altos opposite him, and everybody in that chapel knew it was a proposal. It was three years after his first wife died, after he'd nursed her for over twelve months.'

His mother loved his dad's pure tenor voice, but approaching the house, where he lived till he went to Leeds, he thought of another song he heard on the radio with his mother, when he was twelve, and they were both in the kitchen looking through the window at his dad digging in the garden. It was when she was sleeping in her own bedroom, so she could have a light and the radio on. Ella Fitzgerald was singing *Someone to Watch Over Me,* his mother matching Ella note for note till the end of the song, when he saw the tears running down her face. His dad coming into the kitchen carrying a lettuce and some spuds, she put her arms around his neck to kiss him full on the lips.

'Why, Jeaney, my love,' he said, happily surprised.

I wouldn't be here, if my mother hadn't married him, Warne said to himself, standing in the lane at the back of the house and looking over the low fence to see the house entirely strangled by brick paving for cars and a caravan. I'm me, who married Clarice, because Christopher Farmwell-Pembury raped my mother, and she married 'Flagger Bill', whose first wife died of motor-neurone disease.

'I don't think I've ever got over the rows with my father,' Howard Willetts confessed, after a recent game of squash. 'They were ages ago, but I'd love to bring that past back and make peace with him.'

'I'm reliving the past every day,' he replied. 'It's when Clarice was alive. Anyway I'm paid to unravel it, and in my line of work it doesn't come back with much you want to hear about.'

Occasionally, he glanced through Atherstone's website; people from the town, living all over the world, clinging to memories.

How many of them had the equivalent of a mother raped and a wife murdered?

25

He phoned Manchester CID, asking for Chief Inspector Harry Irvine, a contact from a couple of years ago, when they met on a day's course about data storing and protection. He was told Irvine was just leaving.

'Harry, can you give me half an hour. I can be with you in thirty minutes.'

'That's an hour altogether, David. It's Saturday afternoon.'

'It's important, or I wouldn't ask. I'm only up here for the weekend. I'm back in Canterbury, Monday.'

'Half an hour, max.'

On the train he phoned Jane at Pendlebury Plumbers, saying he'd be late back at her house. She said she'd collect him from Manchester CID.

Lucky City and United are playing tomorrow, he thought, knowing Irvine was a City season-ticket holder.

'You stuffed Liverpool, 2-1, at Anfield last week,' he said, as soon as he and Irvine had shaken hands, and wanting Irvine to be helpful.

'Aye, but your lot's going to win the Premiership again,' Irvine countered.

'You beat us 3-1 in November,' Warne reminded him, and drew with us at Old Trafford, not bad for your first season back in the Premiership.

'You've really no bleeding idea what it's like to be a City supporter,' Irvine insisted, as if determined to be unconsoled.

'Every weekend, all my dad, me and my brothers know is that on Monday we'll have United fans wondering if we're even worth two fingers.' Then he said 'But you look like shit. What's happened?'

Sliding Polly Aldred's envelope onto Irvine's desk, Warne reported what aunty Lucy had revealed.

'Whatever forensics come up with, we won't get anywhere just on what we've got here,' Irvine reflected, tapping the envelope, after having listened carefully. 'The only way is to leak something to the media, see if any other women turn up, more recent, and more likely down South, a job for you. This Sir Christopher's not so well known up here nowadays. But if you start a ball rolling, I can come in with anything forensics finds and, who knows, there might be other women up here too. Rapists who get away with it are likely to rape again. Humiliating women turns the bastards on. You create a stir, and I'll send someone down to interview the fucker, and he won't have the right to refuse us his DNA. It's the only way you'll get some justice for your mother.'

'You look terrible,' Jane said, as he slumped into her car.

'Wait till we're back at your house,' he said, thinking, ends justify means, 'Noble Cause Corruption,' and hearing himself shout 'Bollocks' into Pawsey's face, when Pawsey used the theory to defend his association with Maurice Sewell.

No shouting 'Bollocks' at Irvine.

No rest till Sir Christopher Farmwell-Pembury was as broken and humiliated, as his mother had been.

In the house, each of them with a whisky and some nibbles, he told Jane what aunty Lucy had revealed about his mother and the other women.

'My God,' she said, 'your poor mother, and the others, all degraded. And you, as if you haven't enough to bear already.'

'That bastard solicitor would have been no good for my mother, even if he had married her.'

'No. She escaped him.'

Needing to feel a hit of relief, he poured himself another whisky, a double. Jane was only just into her first.

'You're crying out for comfort,' she said, as he nearly emptied his glass. 'Come on.'

Taking his hand, she kissed him and led him towards the stairs. On the landing she left him to find his own way to the bedroom.

'I really just want to hold you.' he said, when she re-appeared in a robe. He was sitting on the bed in his underwear. 'Nothing more for now.'

'For as long as you want,' she smiled.

26

He woke in her arms, the side of his face resting on her bare breast.

'Well timed,' she murmured, kissing him. 'Remember, I've booked a restaurant, Italian.'

'I'm going to need all the pasta I can get,' he sighed, rolling her on top of him.

'Oh, Oh, Oh, yes,' she gasped as he slid into her.

'I want to stay inside you forever.'

'Oh, it's so lovely.'

'For me too.'

Two hours later, in the restaurant, he was hearing, '*Signora* Scott! *Signora* Scott!', his pasta accompanied by an irresistible *Chianti*.

'I think I've something interesting to tell you,' Jane said, when they were both into their second glass.

'Yeah?'

'I've been having my P.A. look into Marilyn and Bermuda. You remember, a Saudi took her to Bermuda and bought her the penthouse in Manchester.'

'Yeah, I remember.'

'You know what was going on in Bermuda, while she was there in July 1988?'

'Tell me.'

'*Al-Yamamah*, a huge arms deal with the Saudis for oil. According to my P.A., who should have been in your line of work, it's thought to have been the biggest UK sale of anything to anyone, with millions of pounds swilling around in a slush fund of sweeteners.' Sipping her wine, she added, 'Some of that fund paid for Marilyn as a sweetener, and for the Manchester penthouse.'

Marilyn shagging for Britain, he thought, before saying, 'There's been stuff in *The Guardian* about *Al-Yamamah*. It's Arabic for "The Dove".'

'It set Marilyn up financially.'

'So she could move up to Manchester and be ready with a squad of girls when the Premier League came along; young, fit, very rich footballers, with time on their hands most afternoons.'

As she took some more wine, he added, 'Does it bother you to hear that?'

'I'm over it. It doesn't matter to me anymore.'

'Tory government and Labour unions in bed with each other for arms sales and jobs,' he continued. 'Drunken brawls in town centres at the weekend, everybody's outraged. "Where's the police?" Slaughter in distant lands by weapons we've made and sold, who gives a toss, as long you can make an instant coffee, do the school run, and pay the mortgage?'

Not somewhere Jane wanted to go. Running a plumbers business in Manchester, what could she do about the international way of the world? *Al-Yamamah* was only interesting to her, because Marilyn was involved.

A realist?

Get used to it.

'So what about you and me?' she asked, as their deserts were laid before them.

Instantly, as if he'd only been waiting for her to ask him,

he replied, 'I'm finished as a copper. Once I've got everything sorted; what happened to my mother, Marina, Sewell back inside, that's it.'

'Oh!'

'There, I've said it. A relief. I've told nobody else. I've kept a normal surface, but I've been breaking up ever since Clarice was killed, and now there's all the other stuff. I don't want any more of the world I'm in. I've more than paid my dues in it. What everybody sees as entertainment on TV, and reported in the news, that's been my life: corruption, violence, killing.'

'Poor you,' she said, covering his hand with hers. 'What will you do?'

'I'd like to live up here with you. You make me happy again, as happy as I'll ever be. There it is. I've said it, a proposal without a ring.'

Squeezing his hand, she was thrilled, 'You don't need a ring. There's nothing I could want more. Why shouldn't we both have what we want?' Her hand remaining on his, she added, 'Life may change for me too. There's a national company wants to buy me out. They're plumbers' merchants, seeing me as a model for how they might develop if they actually employ plumbers.'

With his arm around her he fell asleep in the taxi back to her house and again, as soon as he was holding her close in her bed.

Next day they went to Liverpool to watch United play Everton at Goodison Park, the last match of the season, United already Premiership champions for the eighth time, but Everton needing to win to have a chance of being in Europe next season. It was Jane's first ever professional football match and, encouraged by Warne, she'd acquired two tickets through one of her plumbers, a United fan.

'Mass identity,' Warne said, aware of her amazement at the passions released all around them. 'Week after week people find or lose themselves in it; like a religion, something bigger than yourself.'

Or smaller, he thought, less than you wanted to be, remembering standing with Clarice at Old Trafford, when they were students; their afternoon destroyed by volleys of racist and homophobic venom directed at Norwich's Justin Fashanu.

As if Clarice were still by his side, he turned to Jane just as she rose instinctively to her feet to cheer wildly with the Evertonians. Kevin Campbell had scored and put Everton in front.

'Come on,' she said, glancing down at him, believing you cheered every achievement on the pitch.

'I'm a United fan,' he insisted, rising just to stretch his legs. 'I want United to win.'

'Oh, I'm not bothered who wins. I'm enjoying it all. That Wayne Rooney playing for Everton looks as though he should still be at school.'

'He's seventeen, already a full England international.'

'And Beckham, with his hair-band and highlights.'

'He may be on his way to Spain.'

But not before he equalised for United with a magical free-kick. And not before Van Nistelrooy won the game for United by diving and winning a penalty.

Everton fans incensed, cursing, helpless.

Jane alarmed, frightened.

Justice hit and miss as much on a football pitch as anywhere else; part of the game, part of life. Everton's big European money gone, as surely as if someone had robbed the club safe.

After the game Jane drove him along the East Lancs Road, a road he used often on his first motor bikes, directly back to Piccadilly station. City had lost one nil at home to Southampton and finished ninth in the Premiership. Maybe enough for Harry Irvine.

'Let's be together, soon,' Jane urged with her final kiss on the station platform.

'Bank on it,' he said.

27

He phoned Pawsey from the train.
    'I'm coming to see you tomorrow afternoon.'
'Fuck me. Says who?'
'Says me. I want everything you've got on Sewell and Sir Christopher Farmwell-Pembury, all the money-laundering.'
'Barbara will be here.'
'She can listen in.'
But all prepared for him, she led him down the garden to Pawsey's spacious greenhouse, so warmed by the May sunshine that all its windows were open. As orderly as if in a TV gardening show, it stretched across the end of the lawn. Waiting for the certainty that the death-threat of frost was ended for another year, healthy cuttings and other tender plants loaded the shelves.
'Tea from me, or tea from Barbara?' Pawsey asked. 'You'll get cake from Barbara.'
'I'll bring the tea,' Barbara said.' It's the only way David will have a clean cup.'
'Once I'm in this place I've everything I need,' Pawsey sighed, when the two of them were alone. He indicated a table, above which were electrical sockets, and on which rested an electric kettle, mugs, a tea container, a jar of instant coffee, a plastic bottle of milk, a larger plastic bottle of water, an open tin of biscuits, and a radio. 'Sometimes I'm here all day, in my own world, nursing these plants, napping on this lounger, pissing

on the compost heap, lungs no problem. Every group Barbara belongs to has raffles for funds, and raffles need prizes. Better win my plants than a bottle of wine you might as well use for cleaning paint brushes.'

'The real me,' he was saying; 'good citizen; forget the Met.'

As if substantiating her husband's claim to a model life, Barbara came back, carrying a tray on which there were two cups and saucers, a tea-pot under a cosy, a tea-strainer resting on a tiny dish, a jug of milk, a plate of home-made cakes, side-plates, spoons, dessert knives, and linen serviettes.

Performing like Lady Penelope, Warne thought. Does she know anything about her husband's corruption?

'Your new boss's wife's an intelligent woman, you know,' Clarice said, when she first met Barbara in the eighties. It was after a drink Pawsey organised in a pub for the four of them; partly so Barbara could interrogate Clarice about Shakespeare's four great tragedies which her reading group was tackling.

He watched Barbara's curvaceous, confident, figure return to the house, as he drank the real tea and bit into a delicious slice of cake.

'Where's Sewell?' he said, when she was out of sight. 'Where's Marina Scott's body, and what are you covering up about Sewell and that bastard Farmwell-Pembury? I know Sewell used him for money-laundering?'

He was sitting on a hard bent-wood, Pawsey in his padded lounger arranged as an arm-chair, as if enthroned in a retirement home.

'So you know about Maurice and the knight,' he responded, ignoring the first two questions. 'Maurice had him by the balls, simple as that; guaranteeing his debts in Aspinall's gambling clubs, where he was mixing with dukes, earls, and cabinet ministers.'

'What else?'

'They were both shagging Marilyn Scott.'

'What! Bank of England man, one of Mrs Thatcher's matinee idols, sharing a whore with Sewell! Sewell must have had more than his balls. He must have had his entire tackle. And Marilyn, Jesus! Legs always open for the big money.'

'Maurice wanted her legs open only for him. He wanted to marry her.'

'Marry Marilyn! '

'Smitten, poor bleeder; his first love dead giving birth to his son, his second wife not up to much.'

'Why didn't they hitch up?'

'Because she wanted to marry the knight; lift the two of them out of all the crap; leave the country, romantic hideaway, real fucking love story.'

'She must have been crazy. Didn't she know the media would be all over them, hunting them down, never letting go.'

'The knight knew. Anyway he loved his show-house and show-life in Kent, "Sir Christopher and Lady Penelope Farmwell-Pembury."'

Warne bit into his cake.

'So then Marilyn has somebody's baby?' he said. 'Whose? It doesn't make sense.'

'Fuck me, Davy boy, somebody's baby! Whose? I thought you were a bleeding detective. It's staring you in the face. It was the fucking knight's baby, Marilyn trying to trap him into marrying her!'

'No! I've a photo of Marina Scott when she was twenty.

She looks just like Marilyn, nothing like Sir Christopher Farmwell-Pembury.'

'Get another photo. Maurice had the full DNA done on the baby and on himself. He wanted a match, wanted the baby to be his, because he wanted Marilyn. Then he got the knight's DNA and knew who the real father was.'

'So Marina was just her mother's bargaining chip.'

'Some part of Marilyn might have thought she actually wanted a child, but the knight always wanted an abortion, and Marilyn was soon desperate to get the thing out of her body with a private caesarean and lots of after-care to smooth her back to how she'd been. All paid for by the knight.'

Useless IVF for Clarice and me, Warne thought. How much we wanted a baby.

'Money all through the girl's education,' Pawsey went on, 'everybody's mouth taped up, but Maurice always turning screws, so no fucking peerage for the knight.'

'I thought he turned the peerage down.'

'Barbara and me saw him saying that on television; no fucking way. Maurice threatened to expose him if he accepted it.'

'Marilyn never shacked up with either of them again?'

'Maurice drew a line. He set her up with a sheik, who took her to Bermuda and paid her enough, so she could move out of the way to Manchester.'

Warne finished his cake and drank more tea. Pawsey drained his own cup.

'The knight was in Bermuda himself,' he said, 'fronting up for the government in that big oil and arms deal, looking the part as a fucking "Sir". But Marilyn and him couldn't afford to even recognise each other.'

'Christ the bastard's everywhere! Did Sewell know whose daughter he was having killed?

'Yeah.'

'Revenge?'

'For his son. He didn't give a shit she was the knight's daughter.'

'Not bothered she was Marilyn's daughter, feelings for Marilyn?'

'Dead and buried. Marilyn didn't care for the girl, so why should he? Why shouldn't he follow the rules of his game?'

'Rules of his fucking game!' He stood up from his chair. 'Murdering a young women; murdering my wife!'

Pawsey went white.

'You don't say things like that on my property, Davy boy.'

'Why not? They're true. All this fucking house and garden, Barbara, your daughters, you've let Sewell kill and maim to pay for the whole fucking lot.'

Pushing up from the lounger, Pawsey immediately collapsed down into it again, as Warne, nearly head-butting him, yelled into his face, 'You're as much of a monster as Sewell. You should be put away.'

'The girl,' Pawsey gasped, cowering in his lounger, and wanting to placate Warne, 'she'll be somewhere, where she can be used. But I swear to God, I've no idea where Maurice is.'

28

As soon as he was out of the house, he called Jane.

'Marina's father was Sir Charles Farmwell-Pembury,' he said almost immediately.

'What!'

'I've as good a source as you can get. That photo in your house of Marina, when she was twenty, have you got any others? Did Marilyn never mention Sir Charles?'

'Never, but I didn't see her a lot, and I've taken no notice of the Farmwell-Pemburys for years. The only other photos I've got of Marina are when she was about ten, and when she was a baby.'

'Send them all to me.'

'If she was his daughter, what does it mean?'

'Bad news for him, if it gets out.'

'Everything about Marilyn getting out too. Her funeral was a quiet affair. It was all about cancer. God, has all this been worth it?'

'You and me?'

'I'm holding on to you and me.'

'Me too.'

No doubt about Marina's father, when Warne saw the photo of her at ten years old. He was Sir Charles Farmwell-Pembury. Pre-puberty she was just like him.

Time we had it out, Warne decided; him and me in the library, just the two of us; especially now his wife's more or less moved in with Gillian and Angela Hartmann.

He was at Nystole Wednesday afternoon, the door opened by the girl who served the coffee weeks ago.

'Hello, I don't know your name.' he said.

'Kylie, Kylie Foster.'

'Live in, Kylie?'

'Best room I've ever had. We've only two bedrooms at home, and I've two brothers.'

'Glad to have your own space, I'll bet.'

'Not arf.'

She showed him into the library.

Sir Christopher was already on his mark at the window, as if ready to shoot the next scene in the film of his life, but sitting on one of the chesterfields was a character Warne didn't expect; Cunningham, in full uniform!

'Sir Christopher invited me, Warne,' Cunningham began. 'Make sure everything's in order.'

Gesturing for Warne to take a seat, Sir Christopher said, 'What is it you wished to see me about, chief inspector?

Ignoring the offer of a seat, Warne moved to stand by the book shelves leading to the window. Immediately at his eye-line on his left, he noticed what might be a metre of *The Dispatches of Field Marshall the Duke of Wellington*, leather-bound. Across the room, over Cunningham's shoulder, the IT equipment emitted its lights.

'I thought my daughter's trial was well in hand,' Sir Christopher continued, 'and you will know the Mitcham family are not being helpful.'

'I'm not here about Gillian,' Warne said.

Sir Christopher stared fixedly through the window into the

clear blue May sky.

'I'm here about another daughter of yours, Marina Scott; a daughter you had in 1976 with Marilyn Scott, a prostitute you shared with the criminal, Maurice Sewell. You'll know about the manhunt for him. It's all over the news.'

'What on earth are you talking about?'

Sir Christopher turned to Cunningham, expecting him to intervene, but Cunningham suddenly looked as if he wished he wasn't there.

More here than this arse-licker bargained for, Warne said to himself.

'I'm talking about a daughter you never acknowledged, but paid for all the way through university,' he went on. 'She was here in Canterbury, right on your doorstep. Didn't you know that?'

'You're living in a fantasy. I never had such a daughter.'

'We'll prove it's no fantasy. Here's a photo, when she was ten. She's just like you. *Look* at it!'

Sir Christopher made no motion even to touch the photo.

'I'll leave it here on this table for later. You can show it to your wife.'

Sir Christopher jerked his gaze away from the blue sky, the sudden fury in his face reminding Warne of Pawsey.

'You scum, how dare you bring your gutter world into my house! I've had Cunningham here look into you and your Labour Party socialism. Marching in London. Attacking me and mine. That's what this is all about. Your working class envy. We'll see to it you're ruined, kicked out of the force, blacklisted.'

Without looking at it, he snatched the photo from the table, tearing it into tiny pieces, while exclaiming contemptuously to

Cunningham, 'This is all there is, a photo to prove a connection with my family! It's a pathetic Anastasia story.'

Watching him put the pieces of the photo into his trouser pocket, Warne said, 'We've at least a dozen copies of the photo, and we're going to find Maurice Sewell. He did the DNA and discovered the daughter was yours, when he wanted her to be his. It meant he and Marilyn Scott always had a hold on you. It's why you couldn't accept a peerage from Mrs Thatcher; nothing to do with all that horse-shit about not wanting one.'

Sir Christopher flinched.

'Where is this daughter? Where's the mother?'

'Both dead.'

'Dead!' Sir Christopher began to look triumphant with relief. 'Assistant chief constable Cunningham will note it's my word against Maurice Sewell, my word against a lifelong criminal, a murderer.'

'He has the girl's body hidden somewhere. We'll find it and do the DNA again. And there's more.'

'More? What do you mean more? How can there be more?'

'Historical sexual assault, rape of young women, who were your employees at Prospero's, the cotton-mill in Atherstone, the town we both come from.'

Sir Christopher gripped the table.

'We have Polly Aldred and Mildred Pomfret, two of your victims at Prospero's, both still alive and aching to testify. Polly Aldred kept the ten quid you gave her in the original envelope. They're with Manchester CID, along with the knickers you tore off her. Forensics has the lot. Any recoverable DNA and fingerprints on the envelope and the pound notes will be yours, and the knickers are stained with her blood and what's likely to be your semen. You sodomised these women.'

Seeming to shrink within himself, Sir Christopher gripped the table more tightly.

'Jean Roberts,' Warne said, moving to within a metre of Sir Christopher and, emphasising each word, 'my mother.'

Sir Christopher appeared to stagger on the edge of a chasm.

'Slim, dark-haired, a trainee office-girl, engaged to Geoffrey Carswell, who became a big solicitor in Atherstone. After you raped her, she had a complete breakdown, and Carswell dumped her. She's dead now, but that bastard's still alive, and I'm going to make sure he testifies under oath on a witness stand. He was your fucking pimp, *for my mother!*'

'Get out of my house.'

'No problem. The problems are all yours, Sir Christopher. Next time I see you, I'll be nicking you. We'll have found Sewell and your daughter's body. We'll likely have more recent rape victims to add to the women from Prospero's. I'll come with the handcuffs myself and a media circus. I'll invite assistant chief constable Cunningham in his uniform. Then we'll see who's fucking scum.'

29

But he saw the owner of Nystole again sooner than he expected. Half-past two Friday morning, the phone challenged his unsettled sleep.

'Yeah!'

'Sorry, sir, Sergeant Baker here. Young girl's just arrived at the station on her bike. She says you'll know her. Kylie Foster, local girl, lives at the Farmwell-Pembury place, Nystole House. She tried to phone, but the signal's no good at Nystole. She says Maurice Sewell's there, been there since yesterday. '

'Christ! Keep her safe. I'm on my way. Tell DS Ozeoke-Bruce to come in. Rustle up the armed response mob.'

He was at the station in fifteen minutes. Kylie Foster was sitting with a WPC.

'Kylie, you're sure it's Maurice Sewell,' Warne greeted her.

'Certain. I saw him last night at eight o'clock. He's in top rooms in the attic. I went to bring dirty dishes down from outside the door. Just as I was picking them up, a great big man holding two beer glasses opened the door. That's when I saw Maurice Sewell along the corridor. I recognised him from pictures on the telly.'

Eddy Barnes, Sewell's latest minder, Warne thought.

'How many are up in the attic?'

'Only two, I think.'

Liz came in.

'Armed response are dealing with an incident in Dover,' she

said. 'Some of them are on their way to us. I've organised paramedics in case there's violence.'

'We better get out to Nystole now,' Warne said. 'Sewell might have seen Kylie leave. He could scarper. Once he's out of Nystole, there's all sorts of tiny lanes we could lose him in. Tell Baker I want anybody he can contact to be here in the next fifteen minutes; everybody wearing full protection and carrying whatever they've been trained for. Kylie, you've been great. Stay at the station. We'll look after you.'

In twenty minutes they sped off in two cars to Nystole; Warne, Liz and five others.

A posse, Warne thought.

At the house, lights and engines switched off, the cars crunched onto the edge of the surrounding gravel. Crouched behind his vehicle and sighting along his weapon, a single armed response officer greeted them.

'This was my day off,' he said. 'Anyway he's waiting for you.'

He nodded towards Nystole's illuminated porch, thirty yards away. There Warne saw Sewell in his black track-suit, shaven head and silver cross gleaming. In red he'd be a cardinal, he thought, checking out the bodyguard, who was in T-shirt and shorts and holding an automatic weapon, and then fixing on Sir Christopher Farmwell-Pembury, in pyjamas and dressing gown, kneeling on all fours like a dog at Sewell's feet, Sewell drilling a hand-gun into the base of his skull.

'He's a sitting duck. I could take him out now,' the armed officer said.

'No,' Warne ordered. 'He's got a gun to Sir Christopher's head.'

'He'll be dead before he can even think of squeezing the trigger.'

'No bloodbath. I want everybody arrested.'

'Suit yourself.'

'I'm going to talk to him.'

'Sir!' Liz said.

'I need information, Liz. If they shoot at me, kill the lot of them.'

Indicating he was unarmed he walked to within twenty yards of the porch.

'You took your time,' Sewell greeted him. 'I saw that girl pedal off.'

'You're coming back inside, Maurice. Let's do it without any mayhem, so nobody gets hurt.'

Two more vehicles arrived; armed officers, paramedics.

'Odds in your favour,' Sewell said, 'a stacked deck.'

'For God's sake, Maurice,' Sir Christopher groaned, 'give yourself up.'

'Shut your fucking mouth, Chrissy.'

'Ah,' Sir Christopher cried out, as Sewell's gun pushed his head lower.

'Everybody calm,' Warne said. 'I've got questions for Sir Christopher too.'

'Sir fucking Christopher,' Sewell mocked. 'Do you hear that "Sir", Chrissy? But you've never really been more than a fucker, have you? Couldn't keep it in your bleeding trousers.'

'Turn yourself in,' Warne insisted.

Considering a moment, Sewell said, 'Eddy's coming in.'

'Boss!' Eddy protested.

'Do as you're told, Eddy. Do your time. Lift your weights. You'll be looked after, and your wife and kids. Give me that weapon.'

Warne watched Eddy reluctantly hand over his weapon, the same as the ones held by the armed officers behind him.

'Treat him nice,' Sewell said, as Eddy, T-shirt packed with body-builder's muscle; neck, arms and legs laced with tattoos, walked past Warne.

Leaning the automatic weapon against the porch, Sewell stretched his left arm towards Warne and sighted along his forefinger.

'You'll get yours,' he said. 'Remember?'

'You murdered my wife.'

'Took away what you loved; same as happened to me with my wife, Gina.'

'She died having a baby. Nobody murdered her.'

Sewell grasped the cross, extending it on its thick chain towards Warne. 'Except what Eddy calls "'im upstairs",' he said. 'He made it happen.'

'God!' Warne exclaimed, incredulously.

'Love or power,' Sewell pronounced, as if in a Credo. 'I was never allowed love.'

'Wasn't allowed!'

'Had to nearly kill my dad, when I was seventeen, so he wouldn't kill my mum. Watched Gina die, so Paul could live. He looked just like her, moved just like her. Then that fucking girl, this cunt's daughter, thinks *she* can take on the world, and he's smashed in pieces under a train.'

'Where is Marina Scott? Where's the body? I need proof she's Farmwell-Pembury's daughter.'

'Proof! She's yours all right, ain't she Chrissy?'

He pushed Sir Christopher's head till his face touched the flagstones of the porch.

'Fucking Marilyn, a top whore; on top of her, on top of the world, till she told him he'd knocked her up.'

'Shoot me now,' Sir Christopher gasped. 'For God's sake, finish everything.'

'What's going on?' A yell from the armed police pack.

Warne watched the question register on Sewell.

'You hear them,' he said. 'What's it going to be, Maurice?'

'The girl,' Sewell said, ignoring the question. 'She's under the swimming pool at the Maltings.'

'Dear God!' Sir Christopher whimpered.

'Dear God!' Sewell echoed, contemptuously.

'Let him go,' Warne said.

'Dear God. No God,' Sewell proclaimed, holding the cross outstretched on its chain.

Then, lifting the chain over his head, he tossed cross and chain towards Warne's feet, declaring, 'You have this shit. It's no good to anybody, just a decoration.'

Raising the hand-gun from Sir Christopher's head, he pushed the short fat barrel into his mouth, thought a moment, before squeezing the trigger and blasting himself backwards into the porch.

Instantly, Liz, the armed squad, and paramedics were at the scene.

From the ground Sir Christopher turned to Warne, slowly raising his hands to accept the cuffs Warne brandished, as if they were a lifeline.

'Let him get up first,' Liz yelled.

But Sir Christopher was never to get up again. Suddenly mumbling incoherently, his body twitching, he collapsed onto his face.

'Jesus, he's having a stroke,' one of the paramedics said.

'No! Stop him!' Warne cried out. 'Don't let him get away with it!'

30

He phoned Jane just before noon. Maurice Sewell was in the mortuary, Sir Christopher, capable only of moving his eyelids, was in hospital.

'I'm coming to Canterbury straightaway,' she responded. 'I'll take a week off.'

'Stay with me. I need you. '

'I'll always need you.'

'Marina will have to be identified.'

'By me!'

'I'll be with you.'

So strange to be in the house with her, sleeping with her in a spare bedroom, facing her, as she sat in Clarice's chair at the breakfast table; as if the drama of his life had been abruptly re-cast, someone else playing the woman in it, someone who would never know the lines already spoken by Clarice, unless he reported them to her; continuity merging with change, and he wanting to hold on to both.

On Wednesday morning they broke through the vivid blue tiles at the deeper end of the Maltings swimming pool and found find Marina Scott's body about a metre and a half below their surface.

'Assuming it's her, we'll unwrap her in the lab,' Sarah Barnes, the pathologist said to him, as the body, parcelled in black plastic and gaffer tape, was carefully lifted onto a stretcher. 'You'll be there?'

'Sure.'

'Try not to remember your wife.'

'I can't help it.'

He attempted to distract himself by thinking about the media and the field-day the tabloids were having. Already, they had more details than he'd revealed at the press conference.

Who told them?

'Anybody in a uniform can be bought, your honour,' echoed in his mind from Sewell's trial.

Not Liz and not me, he insisted to himself, as he left the Maltings, pushing through the pack of reporters and wondering about the uniformed PCs supposed to be keeping the pack at bay.

The tabloids were revealing Marilyn Scott was actually named after Marilyn Monroe!

'How do they know?' Jane cried out over breakfast, when the story was reported in the Today Programme's review of the papers.

'You're telling me it's true? When we were lads, we always thought about her and Marilyn Monroe, but we didn't know there was a real connection.'

'Dad was mad about Marilyn Monroe. He was in her fan club and had a couple of shelves of books and magazines about her. They were nearly the only books in the house, apart from a Bible and an old atlas of the British Empire.'

Fantasies of a bald-headed postman; a Good Samaritan all over his postal round.

'Our Marilyn hated that photo of Marilyn Monroe with her dress blowing up, showing her underwear,' Jane continued. 'When I was about fourteen, she tore it out of dad's book and ripped it up. He was nearly crying. "You want me photo'd, like that," she shouted at him, "saying I want nothing more than to have my knickers pulled down by the first man who walks past!".'

'A grown woman infantilised by men for men,' was Clarice's verdict on the famous publicity shot.

In readiness for the warm day, Jane was wearing a floral skirt, reminding him that Clarice hardly ever wore skirts. She protested about bike leathers, but maybe she found a security in them, and even a kind of triumphalism. No-one else among their friends, man or woman, had ever cruised along an auto-bahn on a motor-bike at ninety miles an hour.

Howard Willetts' under-dressed students came into his mind, as Jane continued, 'Our Marilyn, you know, was a wonderful swimmer, much better than me. She and the water seem to welcome each other, and dad thought he could train her to swim for Great Britain. But she'd given up the training, when she quarrelled about the photograph. And when she was seventeen, nearly eighteen, and almost fully developed and spending nights away from home, she had a terrible row in the front room with dad. I heard her telling him, "The only reason for wearing a bathing costume is so you can have a man on heat like a dog, exactly where you want him". And that time, he really did cry.'

'He always seemed so contented.'

Like all the people crowding the Buttermarket, he thought, as he now made his way from the Maltings back to the station. Through Christ Church Gate he glimpsed the wonderful cathedral. Tourists queued to pay for entrance to it, while outside the pub opposite people sat at tables with their drinks, or squatted on the central war memorial, and a busker sang the Beatles' *Yesterday*. Whatever was happening in Iraq, or anywhere else in the world, whatever was buried under the Maltings swimming pool, or under the surface of their own lives, people in this Canterbury scene were settling for their passing share of happiness, and why not?

I want some of that, he told himself. I want again what I used to have with Clarice.

But towards the end of the afternoon he had to watch with Liz, as Marina was unwrapped from her plastic shroud, and her clothes carefully cut from her.

'For the record, one shot, through the back of the head,' Sarah announced, after she and her assistant had gently turned the body over.

As soon as she was through the door of the safe-house, her killer behind her, he thought immediately, closing his eyes to try to cancel out the horrific vision of Marina helplessly pitching forward, as the bullet blasted into the back of her skull.

A true first.

Did she really believe she could triumph in Sewell's world, where her mother had had to concede and sell herself?

Women always conceding to men?

Didn't you have to concede to someone or something to have a life?

31

Interlacing his fingers with Jane's, he squeezed her hand while she identified Marina, both of them in the mortuary gazing through a screen at the young woman's unreachable stillness.

'You know there'll be an inquest,' he said to her, as they left the building.

'I wish I knew when. I want to bury her with Marilyn, in Atherstone.'

'Marilyn's buried?' He'd assumed she'd been cremated.

'Yes. I didn't want her to disappear entirely, so young.'

'It's likely the body will be released before the inquest, which could be weeks, months away.'

And would reveal, and inquire into, Marina's entire story, he thought: her parentage, her relationship with Jonathan Puttnam, the theft of the money on Eurostar, Paul Sewell's suicide, Pawsey tracking her down, his connection with Maurice Sewell, Sewell having Marina killed, the identity of the killer, and of the burial party at the Maltings.

On the phone Pawsey was ballistic.

'Look what you've fucking done,' he screamed.

'No, look what *you've* fucking done,' he retorted.

'You'll fucking finish me off, Barbara too. We'll have to live somewhere else; start again, at our age.'

'*You* finished Marina Scott off, you evil bastard. You found her in Canterbury and took her to her death. I'd like you done as an accomplice to murder.'

At the end of the week he escaped with Jane to her house, even though the experience included a visit to Marilyn's grave in Atherstone cemetery, the gravestone declaring:

Marilyn Scott

1953-2003

A Precious Daughter, Sister, and Mother

Always Remembered

'Precious … Mother,' he wondered, as Jane said, 'Mum and dad were cremated, like most people nowadays.'

'Same with Clarice's and my family,' he responded reflexively, adding, 'and Clarice and me decided on it for ourselves. It was when we became organ donors.'

Then, out of nowhere, he murmured, '*I depart as air.*'

'What's that?'

'A line from a poem about the end, about returning to the elements; as much as I can say about death. Clarice hadn't heard of it, till I showed it to her. It's from Walt Whitman, American. I was taught at university by a Whitman fanatic.'

'I know nothing about poetry.'

'I don't know much myself, so we're almost the same there.'

The Farmwell-Pembury tombs were nearby, well maintained in an area guarded by strong iron railings and a locked iron gate; principally Sir Christopher's father, grandfather, and great grandfather.

'I wonder if Sir Christopher will be buried with them,' Jane said. 'He still has a brother and unmarried sister who live up here, both younger than him.'

'The sister's moved down to his house in Kent. She's spends

hours by his hospital bedside every day, holding his hand and insisting he knows she's there and is responding. Weird, especially as Lady Penelope's more or less moved in with her daughter, Gillian.'

Then, he said, 'Visiting his tomb in Atherstone, if she ever wants to, will be a long pilgrimage.'

'You don't want to believe she'll want to visit her husband's grave.'

'He raped my mother and two other women up here.'

'Unbearable, I know. Best if Lady Penelope never knew.'

'There's a lot for her to find out,' he said, seeing the anguish in Jane's face and softly kissing her forehead.

Lady Penelope, he was sure, was hearing the voices in the media countering her husband's dealings with Sewell by publicising the good he had had done. Old soldiers under his command in Africa and Italy had been interviewed wearing their medals and saying how easily he mingled with his troops, and how confidently they went into any danger with him. Schools in Atherstone and the surrounding area, and in Kent, had been visited to see various annexes for technical education and for sport that had been built because of his influence and sometimes his money. Surprisingly, Warne learned that when Mrs Thatcher was rampant, Christopher Farmwell-Pembury, as he then was, had argued against the extreme excesses of monetarism, but still she knighted him.

'His friends are speaking of his "tragedy",' he said bitterly to Jane.

'Whatever, it brought us together.'

He saw that for Jane their relationship was becoming all that mattered, especially as it enabled her to find reconciliation.

Always, her instinct was to look for happiness and wish life well. Having voted for Blair, she only regretted he'd bothered with Iraq, because she responded as enthusiastically as the prime minister himself to the millennium's promise of enterprise and endless growth, services, like Pendlebury Plumbers, available whenever you needed them. To Warne's pronouncement, 'Unions regulated, banks deregulated,' she only gave a look of disappointment. During this weekend, she told him how one of her plumbers had had, 'a hernia op, done by some Germans flying into portakabins just off the M60; no waiting in a long hospital queue; in and out and back to work in no time, all on the NHS. What's wrong with that?'

He discovered her plumbers, four of them women, were actually all self-employed.

'Yes,' she admitted, 'they're responsible for their own holiday-pay, sick-pay, and pensions, but so am I for mine. They clear 10K a year more than other plumbers, and all the gear is ready for them on every job they do, all the prices set up, all the accounts settled for them. If I advertised for a plumber tomorrow, I'd have ten applicants the same day.'

New Labour in action, Warne thought; forget traditional allegiances.

Troubled by his persisting doubts, the first thing Jane said to him, when he woke up on Sunday morning, was, 'Morals and business can go together, you know. I got rid of a plumber in January. He hadn't been with us a week. He spent two hours staring into a widow's airing cupboard, tightening one nut, and occasionally banging a spanner on the copper pipes to sound like he was doing something. He charged her one hundred pounds in cash for all sorts invisible work under the floor boards and even drove her to a cash machine. Her son complained to me and took me to his mother's house. I reimbursed her myself. I can't stand cheats.'

Clarice and me, he admitted to himself, while Jane was in the shower, hardly resisted free-enterprise and globalisation. We bought stuff on line from all over the world, ate food and wore clothes produced in God knows what working conditions, rode a BMW bike, drove a Toyota, subscribed to Sky, so I could watch the footy. We weren't Blair's companions in arms, but we went along with him most of the way.

All weekend he felt Jane's pleasure in being with him, as if she couldn't believe her luck, even as she always wanted to remember and honour Clarice.

'Is envy wrong?' she asked. 'I envied Clarice having a man like you. You showed her such consideration.'

'It must have been learned from my dad. He wasn't a "Sir", but he was a true knight to my mum, and to his first wife, I bet. When my mum moved into her own bedroom, he understood that she needed it and set it up for her; though she did regularly move back in with him, much to my pre-pubic curiosity. Clarice admired him no end.'

'I'll always want to share a bed with you.'

'She wants to love and be loved,' he remembered Howard saying of Cindy. He wanted that too, a second time. Weren't Jane's different responses to the world good for him?

And she had other news during this Sunday. The national company intending to take over Pendlebury Plumbers had their sights on her as a chief executive.

'Big responsibilities, big remuneration,' she said. 'My daughter says I should go for it. She says there's so much more I'm capable of.'

'I'm sure there is, but would you have to move from here?'

'No. I can get to anywhere from here.'

'Great.'

He'd been in touch with Manchester University about post-graduate work in criminology. An interview was planned for June. He'd no ambitions in this direction, seeing it simply as something to keep him ticking over. Jane might be taking on a more demanding public life, but he only wanted personal fulfilment with her. He'd had enough of public demands, even though he knew they could never be escaped. *No man is an island*; some more poetry he remembered.

Monday morning, 7.30, before his train home, he was in chief inspector Harry Irvine's office.

'We can't make the forensics work,' Irvine said. 'We can't get a strong enough match between Sir Christopher's DNA and what's on Polly Aldred's knickers, nothing that will stand up in court.'

He looked knackered, envious of Warne's pending retirement and wishing he could retire himself to a life of supporting City and fishing. But he'd four kids, all expecting to go to university.

'You never did leak anything,' he said.

'No.'

'You could still do it, among all this other stuff that's coming out. Other women might show up. Not much chance of him doing you for libel now.'

'He'll be dead as soon as they switch him off. After his funeral, I'll get the two women up here to swear affidavits to be released to the media.'

'Polly Aldred's already got a Manchester solicitor, you know.'

'I didn't know that. What for?'

'Dunno. He's a young thruster. Came to see me with her after you nailed Sir Christopher; making sure nothing's being neglected. I think I convinced them both about the forensics.'

'Some of Sir Christopher's mates are accusing me of vindictiveness, because of my relationship with Marilyn Scott's sister.'

'Mucky world! We both know that.'

32

'Mucky world, mendacious world,' Warne said to Howard, half echoing Irvine before drinking deeply from his pint.

They were in The Bishop's Finger, marvelling over Andrew Gilligan's sensational revelations, on the radio that morning, about last September's government dossier clinching the case for the invasion of Iraq.

Both of them had originally only read summaries of the dossier in *The Guardian*, but both still remembered Tony Blair from TV news on the day the dossier was published. His total command of a specially recalled parliament, as he passionately advocated the case against Saddam and repeated what the dossier, according to Gilligan, stated four times, that Saddam could have WMDs ready in forty-five minutes.

But this morning, Gilligan asserted, via 'a British officer,' that the forty-five minute claim was included in the dossier, even though the intelligence agencies 'thought it was wrong.' In fact, it had never been in the original draft, but was included in the published version 'to make it sexier'.

'Bloody hell!' Warne said, taking another swig. 'Do you believe Gilligan?'

'Well,' Howard responded, sipping his whisky, 'as Gilligan implies, if the WMDs were so ready for use, why haven't they been found? And remember, since last September, we've had another dossier, in February this year. Everybody admits that second one was "dodgy," so why shouldn't we think the first one dodgy too? If WMDs don't turn up, it will be.'

'This war's killing and maiming thousands, more deaths than any criminals cause.'

'Blair's said on TV, he's confident about facing his maker.'

'Fuck!'

'He obviously believes he's doing God's work and will be blessed in a heavenly forum we can never know anything about, except it transcends any court you bring miscreants to. In effect he's granting himself absolution.'

'Jesus!'

'"In God We Trust",' as the Americans say. According to Mark Twain, it's a credo that sounds good and couldn't sound any better, even if it were true. Twain, you know, believed only humour could save us from life's insanities.'

'I must be a humourless sod. I just can't laugh the craziness off.'

'You've not had much of a year for laughs.'

Too true, he thought. He'd fixed up this drink with Howard after an ominous phone call straight after lunch from Irvine.

'Polly Aldred's solicitor's just been on the blower,' Irvine said. 'She's going public.'

'What!'

'They're meeting the media in a couple of hours. No money's involved. She just wants Sir Christopher exposed. Mildred Pomfret won't be there, but she's agreed to be identified as a second victim.'

'And?'

'Your mother won't be named, but Polly Aldred and the solicitor know about her. Don't know how; not from us.'

'It won't be from my aunty in Atherstone.'

'The solicitor's been digging around in the town. I'm sure he's intending to make money, even write a book. Somebody in Atherstone must have always known something, small town like that. Be prepared. Your mother's name's bound to get out.'

'I'm sure my dad never knew.'

'Lucky man.'

Past, past, past, always there, he thought, taking another swig of his pint; the house to sell and nearly all the furniture in it; Clarice's study with about a thousand books, Jane saying she'd never seen so many in a house; still on her desk the last book she'd been reading, a pencil as bookmark; stories of Mary Wilkins Freeman, a writer he knew nothing about; Clarice's comment: 'How MWF likes to equate her apparently insignificant women to great male heroes.'

'United's won the Premiership again,' Howard broke into the silence, obviously wanting to cheer him up. Hardly interested in football, Howard kept up with it for friendship's sake.

'Van Nistelrooy couldn't stop scoring,' he responded, accepting the soft clink of Howard's whisky glass on his larger pint glass.'

'I must remember that name,' Howard said. 'I can use it to appease our Director of Student Experience, Liesebeth van Noortwijk, the next time she wants to persecute me.'

'Is she still on your case?'

'About the semi-naked girls, you mean? No, it's all been dropped. And guess what? The girls are wearing more clothes now than they did all winter. They're both bright, you know. Not as original as Marina Scott, poor girl, but bright enough.'

'Marina wanted to be too original,' he said.

'Always a risk.' Howard drank the rest of his whisky. 'What's going to happen to Jonathan Puttnam? He's phoned me, wondering where his career's going, if it's going anywhere.'

'Dunno about him. I've had bigger fish to fry. I don't wish him any harm. Let's hope the law's lenient with him.'

'As well as more clothes, one of the semi-naked girls now sports a solitaire diamond engagement ring.'

'Good luck to her. Clarice and me, you know, were never officially engaged. She didn't want an engagement ring.'

'Engaged from birth, you two.'

'Maybe.' Finishing his pint, he added, 'I was never sure her mother wanted her to stick with me when we left for university; probably expected her to reel-in an Oxford tosser.'

'But she came back to you.'

'Yeah.'

'Let's both have another,' Howard said, 'and then I'm going to tell you something that will be a shock, but should make you feel good about yourself, and about how much you meant to Clarice and can mean to another person. I hope it will help you move on with Jane, into your new life.'

He went to the bar. Warne went to the Gents.

What could Howard possibly tell him?

He was already at the table with the drinks, when Warne returned, noticing the whisky was a double, which Howard had already started.

'Cheers,' they chimed.

'You know I went to a big academic conference in North Carolina two years ago.' Howard said.

'I'm not sure I can remember.'

'Doesn't matter. But I met someone there called Sheldon

Gebeloff. He was the conference director, and we'd already corresponded. He's a mega wheeler-dealer in modern literature, English and American, and a millionaire several times over. His family owns factories supplying car components to Detroit. Some of these factories have moved down Mexico way.'

'And?'

'Sheldon Gebeloff did his doctorate at Oxford. He proposed marriage to Clarice.'

'What!'

'In her final year. They had a relationship. She turned him down.'

'Come on, Howard. Where's all this from?'

'Him. At the bar one night, we got talking about education, schools. I mentioned this great woman teacher I knew, uncommon name, Clarice. Talk about lighting his fire. He's married with three kids, but if I'd been a magician with a cloak and conjured Clarice from under it, he'd have run away with her there and then. He offered her a fabulous American life, finance her through a Ph.D. at Harvard or wherever. She told him he was too rich, and she couldn't separate herself from ordinary life. She meant you, my old buddy. She preferred you.'

He stood up, raising his glass in a toast to Warne. Then, downing the rest of his whisky in one gulp, as if he was in the saloon bar of a Western, he said, 'Leave you now. Get a taxi home to Cindy.'

Beginning to move unsteadily towards the door, he bumped into the table, causing Warne to grasp his glass with both hands.

So Clarice wasn't always in a nunnery in her final year.

Alone at the table, he began to cry silently, overwhelmed by his love for her, and all the life they had had and lost.

33

He met Jane next day, Friday evening, at the West Station. Under her arm was the *Daily Mail*. He'd already seen its exclusive splash, Polly Aldred's and Mildred Pomfret's stories, together with photos of the two women as young and pretty twenty year olds, and the photo, from Billy Lee's studio, of his mother at eighteen, looking like Ava Gardener. 'Chief Inspector Revenge' was a tabloid's new title for him.

'Reception party!' he said to Jane, as he inched the car through the swarm of reporters and photographers at the entrance to his drive. 'Let us get out of the car, lads,' he yelled through his open window. 'You can have all the photos you want.'

But they wanted more than photos.

'How long have you known about your mother and Sir Christopher?'

'Was Jane ever in London with Marilyn?'

'Was she on Marilyn's books?'

'There's a rumour you're Sir Christopher's son.'

In the house Jane was crying.

'My God, how long will this go on?'

'There may be more spillage about Sir Christopher. We need to get him buried.'

'He's not even dead yet.'

'He should be. His sister won't let him go.'

'I want to bury Marina.'

'I don't know what more the inquest can want from her body.'

During the weekend they attempted relief by discussing practical matters. Jane would inherit all of Marilyn's estate and told him of her plan to use it to build a suite of rooms as an extension to a women's refuge in Manchester, and have the suite named after Marilyn. Revealing more of her instinctive generosity she also proposed he buy half of her house, at very advantageous terms to himself.

'Help finance you through university,' she joked.

'Thanks, though I shouldn't have any money worries. This house is worth a bit, and I've two pensions to draw on.'

As she put her arms around his neck to kiss him, he added, 'A new life with you will always have to be in your place "up North". There's not much passion left in me down here.'

'There's been enough.'

What he'd referred to as 'spillage' poured out during the following week. Responding to Polly Aldred's revelations, two other women, in their late forties, claimed they had been sexually assaulted by Sir Christopher, when they were young secretaries in London.

These stories breaking and others threatening, Sir Christopher's life support was switched off. Pointedly drawing contrasts with the 'coldness' of Lady Penelope, the media showed his grief-stricken sister leaving the hospital on the arm of her other brother.

And during the same week Liz's promotion came through, sending her off, along with Warne's congratulations, to arrest a student drug-dealer at the university.

'He has a Mercedes,' she said, when she returned to the station.'

'He must think he's big-time, having a brand new DI on

his case. Congratulations again, Liz. You've always deserved it.'

And you'll always have more than enough crime to deal with, he thought, remembering Pawsey's fatalism; unstoppable varieties of desire, deviance, self-expression, free enterprise, violence, no matter who's a copper. Already, this morning, before Liz set off for the university, they had a man in custody for exposing himself to school-girls on a bus, a woman for shop-lifting, another man for kicking and breaking the leg of a parking attendant who'd just given him a ticket, and a gang using a JCB to rip cash machines from walls.

Recently, Liz had started talking about Nigeria, as if her police career in the UK was separating her too much from half of her ancestry. She told him she was in touch with a cousin in Port Harcourt about the recent April and May elections.

'Intimidation nearly everywhere,' she said. 'Guns on all sides, vote buying, ballot box stealing and stuffing.'

'You think you should be upholding the law there?'

'I feel guilty because I know I wouldn't be up to it. Whatever the pressures, life's easier here. Corruption's all over sub-Saharan Africa.'

'With the dirty money cleaned up in London.'

This afternoon, sheathed in her new identity as a DI, her self-possession was back.

'You're taking a battering in the media,' she said.

'I'll survive.'

'Maltings' residents want their swimming pool back.'

'Not my problem.'

'Nobody seems to know whose problem it is.'

'Well, you live there, Liz, and you're becoming senior in the police force that wrecked the place. I don't live there, and I'll soon be out of the force.'

'De-mob happy?'

'Nearly.'

34

Days later, at the beginning of June, Lady Penelope made an appointment to see him in his office.

'I wanted to thank you personally, chief inspector,' she said, shaking his hand, before sitting in a not very easy and not very clean chair, while he retreated behind his desk. 'You always showed great consideration towards my family, especially over Gillian and Mark.'

'We'd no idea about the other stuff that came out,' he said.

'It affected you as much as anyone.'

'Yes.'

'Your poor mother.'

'Yes.'

'I want you to know I bear you no hard feelings, no animosity. I reject all the insinuations about vindictiveness and revenge. It will be no help, but I apologise from the bottom of my heart for what your mother, and the other women, suffered.'

'Thank you. It does help actually.'

'I heard an expression on television, "calling out". I should have called my husband out years ago. My sister wanted me to, but I lacked the courage, and I never imagined the crimes he had committed and was committing. Polly Aldred had courage.'

'She's been very determined.'

'Yes, an example to all women. But now I understand you have a new relationship.'

'An old friend from Atherstone. She knew my wife.'

'I'm so glad you have another chance of happiness, like Gillian.'

'We're hoping Gillian gets a light sentence, at worst.'

She did not reply, and he sensed she was suddenly lost within herself, as if wondering forlornly where she might find new happiness.

'Christopher's sister,' she said, as if it would explain something, 'was always in love with him, idolised him; no other woman good enough, that sort of thing.'

What could he say to this?

'But, I mustn't take any more of your time,' she declared, standing up and brushing dust from the chair off her pastel blue silk skirt and jacket, 'though there is one other thing. I intend to come to Marina Scott's funeral. I'd be grateful if you would let me know when and where it will be.'

'It will be in Atherstone.'

'Good,' she replied, offering her hand. 'I'll come with my sister.'

He accompanied her to her car and chauffer, as, weeks ago, he'd accompanied Vincent Clements. Her chauffer opening the rear door for her, he had a strange longing to slide in beside her. Protect her? Why?

He saw her next at her husband's funeral, in Atherstone, at the end of June. Standing with Jane among a clump of spectators and TV cameras, he watched the *cortège* walk from the cemetery chapel to the family tomb: Lady Penelope, Judith her sister, Gillian, Angela Hartman, Caroline, Sir Christopher's brother and family, his weeping sister, MPs, ex-MPs, CEOs, people from Farmwell-Pembury enterprises, Geoffrey Carswell and his wife, the mayor wearing his chain of office, and

Cunningham in his uniform; all following a priest in his robes and with a silver cross, like Sewell's, on his breast; and an altar boy, in surplice and cassock, carrying on its wooden pole, high above his head, the cross from the parish church.

Showtime, he thought, hearing Clarice say, of other public occasions, 'Establishment male theatre.' The whole shebang might crash down if they let one of their own, no matter how disgraced, be buried insignificantly. And the church will always dress up and play its part, if there's a camera around, or the money's right.

Geoffrey Carswell catching his eye, he mouthed 'pimp' at him, but then, as Carswell looked away unflinchingly, he was immediately ashamed, knowing his mother would not want him to exploit her suffering so cheaply.

That evening he watched *Channel Four News*, while Jane was on the phone discussing her new career with the CEO of the company she was joining. He saw the duel between Jon Snow and Alastair Campbell over the government's dossiers making the case against Saddam, especially last September's dossier and its WMD forty-five minutes claim. Campbell wanted an apology from the BBC for its support of Gilligan's contention that the claim was included in the dossier, even though it was known to be false.

This contention was a lie, Campbell asserted.

We do not know that, Snow responded.

An argument for itself, he concluded; about journalism, accuracy of reporting, sources, and what it's politic to reveal; two men locking horns. It's caused by the war in Iraq, but detached from it, the slaughter forgotten; like the funeral this afternoon, it's a performance; like me wanting to perform by chinning Geoffrey Carswell, which I don't want to do anymore.

He saw that the repercussions of any event have lives of their own, become events in themselves, spawn more repercussions and events, till you can't distinguish between the two, and you forget the original, if it even was the original. Who knew the original for the invasion of Iraq?

'It's like trying to work out the first cause of a Shakespearian tragedy,' Clarice said, sharing out the wine during that last dinner in Ypres, 'and you know what? Bush may actually be a cowboy Hamlet, finishing off Saddam on behalf of his father.'

35

There were more repercussions in the middle of July. On the day before Marina was buried, David Kelly, the Iraq weapons inspector exposed and humiliated as a source for Gilligan's challenge to the September 2003 dossier, apparently committed suicide.

Two days before his death, in an unrelenting televised inquisition, he'd been told by an MP he was 'chaff.'

What was Marina, Warne thought, as her coffin was poised to be lowered into the grave, and as Howard, in his tribute, spoke of her 'Fierce determination not to be deceived.' She'd been found, because Jane's loving nature was determined not to lose her from the family. Jonathan Puttman too must have cared for her, and Howard certainly did, whilst he knew her. But she was no more than chaff to her mother and father, and to Pawsey and Sewell, and to whoever put a gun to the back of her head, and to those who wrapped her in black plastic and gaffer tape and buried her at the Maltings.

Which of us, beyond our small circle of love and friendship, is not chaff?

Aunty Lucy, as weightless as a leaf yesterday, when he lifted her from her bed at home, so it could be changed.

Watching the coffin being carefully lowered into the grave, he intertwined his fingers with Jane's. By their side were a tearful Lady Penelope and her sister, Judith. Opposite were Howard and Cindy, and Jane's daughter, Fiona, holding the hand of

Hassan Ernaux, whom she lived with in Paris, and whose mother's family was from Algeria. About half a dozen friends of Jane from Atherstone were also there, and local media.

His handful of soil rattling on the coffin lid, his heart tightened. Again he heard himself telling Clarice, on the last day of her life, 'You always get *la mort.*'

'You OK, my old buddy,' Howard asked anxiously, when he shook Howard's hand and thanked him for the tribute.

'Yeah, and Cindy?'

Her pregnancy was just visible.

A taxi waited at the cemetery gates for Lady Penelope and Judith. It would ease them back to the Midland Hotel in Manchester. They'd declined the meal Jane had arranged in a restaurant.

He shook hands with Judith, then, holding his hand towards Lady Penelope's, also bent forward to kiss her cheek, which she offered willingly, while Judith, her bodyguard, looked on, unmoved by the afternoon's proceedings.

'We should have adopted Marina,' Lady Penelope declared, as she turned to the taxi.

'Mother and daughter together,' Jane said to him, when he was again by her side. 'How much they missed in life. I never want to lose contact with Fiona.'

He knew this final re-union of Marilyn and Marina meant so much to her. Pawsey's defence team, working against accessory to murder, had nearly driven her to despair by having Marina's body re-examined several times.

'Pawsey's had to sell his house to pay for everything,' he told her a couple of weeks ago. 'He's moved to a flat in Darlingon, near to where his wife comes from. It's sure to kill him. He had a garage full of wonderful tools at his house.'

'He means nothing to me,' she replied.

After the meal in the restaurant, Fiona and Hassan, together with Howard and Cindy, were staying the night at her house.

'I'm so glad you're making mum happy,' Fiona said to him, as they all enjoyed a nightcap.

'When I first saw you, you were about eighteen months old,' he responded. 'You were sitting up in your pram, your mum, still looking like a schoolgirl, pushing you.'

'Did you say hello to me?'

'I was on my motorbike with Clarice. We were going camping near Stratford, seeing some plays.'

Triumph Bonneville, he remembered, his second bike, bought by his dad, when his dad was convinced he knew how to handle it; his mother, worried, waving them off; end of their first year at university.

'I hope Jonathan Puttnam comes out of everything OK,' Howard said, joining them with a brandy in his hand. 'He's just had a son. Paternity! It sure changes your outlook.'

'You'll have to play a lot of lullabies,' Cindy said, from the sofa.

And then it was time for bed, Jane snuggling against him in the warm night, her breasts, through her thin top, resting pleasingly against his bare chest.

'Fiona and Hassan are serious about each other,' she said.

'I like what I see of him.'

'I heard you saying to Fiona I looked like a schoolgirl pushing her in her pram.'

'So you did.'

'I'll be fifty soon.'

'Me too.'

'Cindy looks great.'

'Yeah, Howard loves her being pregnant. He can't wait to become a father.'

'You know what they used to say of newly-weds in Atherstone, when they'd settled down after the wedding.'

'No. What?'

'They're going in for a baby.'

'Yeah, I remember.'

'You should have a child, and I'd love to have one with you.'

'Oh, yeah?'

'We should go in for one before it's too late.'

'Oh, yeah!'

Rolling on top of him, her lips caressed his ear. 'I can feel you want to go in for one right-away.'

'Hmm,' he murmured.

THE END

ACKNOWLEDGEMENT

I am happy to thank Keith Carabine, my friend for over fifty years, who delayed his Conrad scholarship to provide very helpful readings of drafts of this novel.

Ah, love, let us be true / To one another", Helena says to Steve, quoting from poetry she teaches. Nothing Steve wants more. From very different backgrounds they work in a university, Steve as Director of the Sports Centre. He'd wanted to be a professional footballer, but became a soldier in Northern Ireland and the Falklands, doing his share of the killing. Life may be 'a loaded gun' Helena tells him, quoting another poem. Britain in the 80s is torn by conflict, and in this political thriller more than one gun is fired.

ISBN 978-1-911546-16-0

Available from www.amazon.co.uk

www.theconradpress.com and all good bookshops